# THE FACULTY OF INDIFFERENCE

GUY WARE is the author of more than thirty short stories, including the collection, *You Have 24 Hours to Love Us*, and three novels. He won the London Short Story Prize 2018 and was longlisted for the Galley Beggars Story Prize 2019. *The Fat of Fed Beasts*, was chosen as a 'Paperback of the year' by Nick Lezard in the *Guardian*, and described as "Brilliant . . . the best debut novel I have read in years." *Reconciliation* was described by *The Literary Review* as "memorable and inventive" and by the *Guardian* as "exhilarating, and very funny". Guy lives with his family in New Cross, South London.

# THE
# FACULTY OF
# INDIFFERENCE

GUY WARE

SALT

CROMER

PUBLISHED BY SALT PUBLISHING 2019

2 4 6 8 10 9 7 5 3 1

Copyright © Guy Ware 2019

Guy Ware has asserted his right under the Copyright, Designs and
Patents Act 1988 to be identified as the author of this work.

First published in Great Britain in 2019 by
Salt Publishing Ltd
12 Norwich Road, Cromer NR27 0AX United Kingdom

www.saltpublishing.com

Salt Publishing Limited Reg. No. 5293401

A CIP catalogue record for this book is available from the British Library

ISBN 978 1 78463 176 5 (Paperback edition)
ISBN 978 1 78463 177 2 (Electronic edition)

Typeset in Neacademia by Salt Publishing

Printed and bound in Great Britain by Clays Ltd, Elcograf S.p.A

*For Sophy*

*And if you have lived one day, you have seen*
*all: one day is equal to all other days. There is*
*no other light, there is no other night.*
—MICHEL EYQUEM DE MONTAIGNE

# CONTENTS

# FOUR OR FIVE YEARS AGO

# FOUR

"HOW WAS IT today?"

Stephen asked that all the time, four or five years ago. Not all the time, obviously. Not all day; not even every day, but most days – most working days – when I got home from the office or, more often, from the pub we drank in when we left the office. He'd ask how it had been. Sometimes, it's true, I'd come home from somewhere else. The office of a partner agency, perhaps, or an investigation site: the scene of an explosion, say, or a shooting. On such occasions, however, the time of my return would be less predictable, and Stephen would be less likely to ask how my day had been, because he might not be in the kitchen, making dinner, or in the living room watching TV, but upstairs, in his own room, working, or writing his journal. Then he might call out hello, but nothing else. Or he might say my dinner was in the microwave (if I were late) or that he'd be cooking soon (if I were early). The day I was describing, though, four or five years ago, he'd asked how it had been, and the following day I said – to Simmons and Leach, not to Stephen – that he sounded like my mother, or Mary.

"That's nice," Simmons said. She liked to give the impression that she saw the best in everyone (which was difficult, sometimes, and probably a disadvantage, in our profession). I said he was my son, for pity's sake. He was not supposed to be solicitous. There'd be time enough for all that when I was too old to tie my own shoelaces. Simmons said it was nice he showed an interest. But we all knew where that might lead. I told them I'd said, How was what? and he'd said: Work, what else could it be?

Leach put down his glass. "Hang on a sec . . . Did you say that or did he?"

"Say what?"

"What you said. About what else it could be."

I looked at Leach – something I try not to do too often. "You want to know if I said what I said ten seconds ago?"

He said I knew what he meant, which of course I did, so I said that I'd said that. Which, if he'd thought about it, wouldn't have left him any the wiser.

Simmons ignored him. She said her daughter, Nicola, didn't even know what she did for a living, much less ask. She said of course she didn't *know*, but, well, we knew what she meant, and of course we did, it was the same for all of us. She said MydaughterNicola, as if it were one word.

This conversation, if it is not already obvious, took place in a pub, after work. The pub in question was the Butcher's Arms, just across the road from the Faculty, from work – so we couldn't talk *about* work, because you never knew who else would be there – and just across another road from the railway station, so we *could* each drink until two or three minutes before our respective trains were due to leave; in other words, it was pretty much perfect, despite its many faults. The place was generally crowded, and smelled less of beer than of the damp, gently poaching fug of nicotine-impregnated overcoats; of acid sweat and twelve-hour-old deodorant; and of cooking, it being the kind of pub that sold food, after a fashion. I suppose they had to make a living. Even at five thirty, when nobody was eating anything more adventurous than crisps, the scent of a crowd dressed for a bitter cold December but crammed into an overheated locker room still carried a subtle note of grilled meat, chips and fake Thai curry. It was a pub none of us would ever have drunk in, not by choice, had it not been a mere grenade's throw from both the office and the railway station. We were not there for the company.

It hadn't been a good day – either the day before, when Stephen asked, or that day itself, the day we were in the pub discussing the fact that he had asked – not a day that any of us would call *a good day* (that would be too much to ask), but it hadn't been a bad day, either. No one had fired a mortar into a cinema; no one had worn a suicide vest to a crowded supermarket; or if they had, it hadn't worked. Which, while not exactly the same thing, was good enough to be going on with.

There was still time, of course. The night was yet young.

Leach said, "So what did you say?"

"What I always say."

"Which is?"

"If I told you that, I'd have to kill you."

Simmons said she – by which she meant herdaughterNicola – was all over her dad, but that was girls for you. Never mind that it was Simmons who paid for all the riding lessons and the field trips to fucking Mauritius.

Leach, a beat behind as usual, said: "Do you mean kill me, or him?"

When I got home, he said it again – How had my day been? – and I said: "Don't." He said he was only asking, trying to be empathetic. I asked if they taught him that at school these days.

He said, "I made spaghetti."

"At school?"

"For dinner."

I said I was sorry, and it wasn't that far from the truth.

He was a decent cook, as it happens, for a boy of seventeen.

Work, meanwhile, had been what it always was: intolerable. When anyone else asked, if I didn't just say I couldn't say because then I'd have to kill them, I would say: You don't want to know. But, really, by then – when I'd already been at the Faculty for twenty years or so – no one but Stephen ever asked, because the only other people I talked to *were* at work (Simmons, Leach, Butler) and they already knew. In the past – ten, fifteen years ago, when Mary was around – there'd been people who persisted, out of misplaced politeness, perhaps. She would invite them to our house, or be invited to theirs. I'd go with her and they'd ask and I would say, no, really, you don't, you really do not want to know.

Intolerable? I'd tolerated it.

While we ate, Stephen said it had happened again. I didn't need to ask – and wouldn't be able to do anything, or even say anything, that would help – but I asked him anyway what had happened again. It gave the semblance of conversation.

"The knocking."

I said, "The same as before?"

He nodded. He said it had been the same, only more so.

Ours was a terraced house and sometimes – on one side in particular, where the chimneys were back-to-back and fed the same flues – you could hear the neighbours breathe. One night, years ago – it must have been – Mary and I had been in bed. She'd rolled off me, and I'd rolled too, and laid my arm across her belly, my face against her shoulder, and watched her breast rise and fall as her breath slowly returned to normal. She reached for her cigarettes, and in that perfect moment we both heard the man next door, in his bedroom, laugh and say, "See?" and his wife say, "No." We hadn't known whether they were talking about us or them, but we'd both laughed, too, laughed uncontrollably, until Mary forced herself to stop and put her hand over my mouth and rolled back on top of me. I knew, too, that soon, in less than two years, Stephen would leave. He would go away to university and I'd have the house to myself with only the sound of the television, the rattling of cutlery in the drawer as I did the washing up, the neighbours coughing, or plugging and unplugging electrical appliances, but in the meantime I had not once heard the knocking Stephen regularly complained about.

I said, "More? Do you mean louder?"

He said he meant *more*, going on for longer, but otherwise just the same. Except that it was never the same, no pattern or repetition, it was just noise.

After dinner we watched the news together. I sat in the armchair, as usual, while Stephen lay across the sofa with his feet – which were already bigger than mine, and bony, and seemed, to be honest, like the feet of some cave-dwelling giant – hanging over one arm of the sofa, the one nearest to me, his head resting on the other. There were hairs growing from his big toes, which did not seem possible, but there they were. After a few minutes, Stephen twitched and reached out for a book on the coffee table, riffled through the pages and put it down again. There was not much in the news. Obviously there were things not in the news, by which I mean things left out of the news, things that I could have told him about, if he were interested. If he had asked about my work today (and every other day) because he wanted to know – not just because he wanted to ask, or rather, to have asked and for me not to have replied – and if it had been possible for me to tell him anything. Things about the threat level, for example: why it was what it was. Instead, I asked what he was reading. Not because I wanted to know, of course, but because I wanted to have asked. He asked about my work, when he shouldn't – that wasn't what teenaged boys were supposed to do, but he did it anyway – and I didn't answer. I asked what he was reading because that *was* what I was supposed to do. I was his father; he was my son. It was my job, my function, to take an interest in his life, or at least to show an interest. He picked up the book again and tossed it across the room to me, inaccurately. I failed to make the catch and the slim paperback – less than two hundred pages, I guessed – hit the wall behind me. I said he shouldn't treat books like that. I picked it up from the floor: Marcus Aurelius' Meditations. If I opened the cover, I would find 'Mary Walsingham' written in pencil on the title page, and the year she'd bought it, if she'd bought it when she was a student, which seemed likely. Walsingham was her maiden name; she sometimes claimed to be descended from Sir Francis Walsingham himself, mostly when she was drunk. She sometimes said it was the only reason they'd let her in the Faculty at all, although nobody believed her. But it might say 'Mary Exley', if she'd bought it after we were married, when we were both already working there and she'd felt the need to remind herself she was an intellectual at heart, a scholar, which happened from time to time. I opened it instead at one of the pages where the corner had been folded down, and read aloud a sentence that had been underlined: *Nobody is surprised when a fig tree brings forth figs.*

Stephen was studying Philosophy – something else they hadn't taught at my school – along with Greek (ditto) and English Literature. I'd done sciences, and read Biology at university. There was little chance that we would understand each other.

I said, "What does that mean, then?"

He shrugged.

"To you, I mean. You underlined it."

Or it might have been Mary.

After a while he shrugged again. "What it says."

I stood up and gave him back the book. He stood up, too, and took it with him up to his bedroom. I wished him good night.

The news was followed by a crime drama. It was a series and I hadn't seen the earlier episodes, but I guessed I'd pick it up without much trouble. From upstairs I could hear the muffled peck – stuttering at first, but gradually growing more fluent, more rhythmic – of Stephen's typewriter.

# 384081074098

384081074098170419749719479147190491749194791094801741 8
220410840917190840179470091490979818094798269828756 20
947872367856209478714872897498349729846829846814098043
70910461093487104697154671573265975027487629871237132719
8570198570975785175583571 09
 4714761947759125923

4579347523479234757194758234579283475234065184370561894517
3457837457083475723489573480819579813459613475923645012395
6158347856890347589726394578346589734503895782630495 71873
450389745719834857983457134578190345789640591798650 74856
82345876234957283645378462 8
 93401523061982765102346120513254612312351059812674612651
20158972319826357127568162457182357109842560918275081627 45
900128705816274058761238956012850182650861285608712645 9081
620865109826598127350862098610856701265 06

# A CROCK OF SHIT

IN THE MORNING, Stephen usually got up before me and would be in the bathroom, doing whatever a seventeen year-old boy can do for so long in a bathroom - not shaving, obviously, or not often anyway - while I went down to the kitchen and prepared breakfast. I made porridge for Stephen, something else I'd never understand. I'd given up offering him eggs. Mary ate avocados when she could get them, bananas when she couldn't, sprinkled with cayenne - and cigarette ash, if she wasn't careful. I made toast, and tea.

I left for work before Stephen left for school, sometimes before he came downstairs, and the porridge would be cooling in the pan; he'd get back in the afternoon long before I did.

It was December, so in the train we all crushed up against each other in our overcoats, each of us leaking sweat and mucus, exchanging body fluids and avoiding eye contact. The train was on time and took no longer than usual, but that was bad enough. Dante, Mary used to say, might have run out of circles if he'd lived long enough to experience our suburban railway network. As we left the station a blind, merciless wind like a surgeon's scalpel whipped off the river, sliced through our clothes and flesh, condensed the air in our lungs and cracked apart our bones to freeze the very marrow deep within. All, in my case, in the three minutes it took to cut between the buses that coughed and shuddered like old men at their stands, to cross the roads around the silent Butcher's Arms and finally reach the blank, unlabelled airlock entrance of Faculty HQ.

On the third floor, Simmons was already at her desk. She was generally the first to arrive. Leach was just as often late because, to be honest, he was a lazy bastard; Butler was the most recent recruit to our team and didn't seem to have that much to do. Maybe Gibbon had been breaking her in gently before he disappeared. She was twenty-seven, twenty-eight, I guessed, with a wide diaspora mouth and something of an overbite, which made her catch her bottom lip between her teeth and seem younger and more gullible than she was. She never came to the pub with us after work. She said she couldn't drink, or watch other people drink. She rode a bicycle, a fold-up contraption she brought into the office, and wore short, stretchy skirts over sixty denier tights. She also had a thing for Leach – Simmons said, and I hadn't really agreed or disagreed – which she had never declared, presumably because she never came to the pub and therefore never reached the condition you'd have to be in to admit to such a thing. That was Simmons' theory, anyway. Perhaps I just wasn't tuned in to the signals. It had been a long time since I'd taken interest in anything like that.

I hung my coat on the stand, but before I could sit down Simmons called me over to her desk. She asked if I would help her out with a case. I asked why she thought her case might be more important to me than any of my own, of which I had no shortage, and she said she didn't. There wasn't any reason. It was just that she was drowning, there was no way she could cope with her in-tray, that now we never saw Gibbon he seemed to be sending the stuff through faster and faster. I asked if she'd asked Leach. She gestured to his empty desk.

"But, if he *were* here?"

We both knew that she wouldn't. She wouldn't have contemplated it for more than a second, if that, because he wouldn't have agreed. And even if he had, she probably wouldn't have wanted him to.

I said, "All right."

When you got down to it, one case was much the same as another.

She gave me the file, which was thick and had the name Volorik hand-written on a white label on the buff folder, the label stuck over three or four other labels as the folder itself had been used and re-used. Inside, there was enough paper-work to keep me reading till lunchtime, but none of it told me all that much, or not much that made sense. When I asked Simmons if she were coming to lunch she said no, she was too busy. Leach said he'd come if I were buying, and Butler, who never came to the pub, but sometimes came for lunch because it didn't involve alcohol (except on the very worst days), said she'd come, too. I shrugged, to indicate that more would be merrier – not a sentiment I'd generally endorse, but if I had to have lunch with Leach, it would leaven the load for Butler to be there too. I asked Simmons if she were sure, but she said she was.

In the café Leach asked what Simmons' case was about, the case I'd taken on for her. The place was crowded, the windows and even the tiled walls fogged with condensation, and we'd had no choice but to share a table. Butler signalled to Leach, gesturing at our neighbours – builders, by the look of their tool belts, boots and the yellow hard hats they'd moved off the seats when we sat down – as if Leach might not have noticed them. He sighed with exaggerated weariness and said, "*Pas devant les civils?*"

Butler gave me a complicit look I took to mean: what *are* we going to do with him? She said, "You think terrorists don't speak French?"

Leach blew froth across the top of his coffee, the coffee I'd paid for, and said: "Nobody speaks French."

"Apart from the French?"

"Apart from the French."

"And the Senegalese," she said. "The Algerians. The Cameroonians, the Haitians." She paused for a moment. "The Canadians."

Leach said, "Like I said."

"Belgians," I said. "Half of them."

"Mauritians," said one of the builders. "I am from Mauritius."

"Guineans."

Leach said, "Is that a word?"

I said, "Tunisians?"

"The Swiss," said a second builder, who probably wasn't Swiss. "Some of them."

"Yeah," I said. "But apart from them?"

"Nobody actually speaks French," said Butler.

"Ha bloody ha," said Leach. "Now we've established that, Exley, what's the case about?"

I sighed. I looked at Butler. I tapped the side of my nose and said, "Fantastic."

"What?"

"Spastic."

Leach said, "I don't think you're supposed to say that anymore."

"It's rhyming slang."

"Rhyming slang? Fuck off."

Butler was gesturing to him to keep his voice down, but the builders were already joining in. "Mastic," one said, in what might have been an eastern European accent.

"Drastic?"

"Elastic?"

"Periphrastic?" That was Leach, who could surprise you sometimes.

"Plastic," said the builder from Mauritius.

"Ah," said Leach.

"Indeed," I said.

"Boom," said Leach.

I nodded. "Boom boom."

"That doesn't work," said one of the builders.

"Yes," said Leach, "it does."

"How?"

"If we told you that," Leach said, "we'd have to kill you."

Butler stood up, "Don't worry about us," she said. "We've got to go."

Outside it was just as cold as it had been on the way in, which is to say cold enough to make you see the point of vodka. Butler said we ought to know better. I couldn't hear her very well through the long woollen scarf she'd wrapped at least three times around her face. Leach said, "You think the walls have ears?"

"*People* have ears, Leach."

I said I wouldn't worry. The truth of it was that Simmons' case – which was now my case, except that it would still be her name on the report that went back up to Gibbon, unless it all went pear-shaped and she found a way to weasel out of it – didn't seem to be about much at all. There was plenty of paperwork, but none of it made sense and, while I hadn't been exactly lying about the explosives – they were all over the file – I wasn't at all sure they actually existed or would be used, if they did exist, for the purpose alleged by the people involved, if they were involved. Which I didn't believe.

On the face of it, then, a crock of shit.

Which might mean it was just that: a crock of shit.

I said, *"Qu'est ce c'est un civil*, anyway?"

T HAT AFTERNOON I made some excuse and took the
lift down to the Crypt, which might have been a floor
or two below ground level, but wasn't actually dark or damp
or spooky. Which didn't mean there weren't ghosts down
there. Some of the rooms were dark, it's true, but not the sort
of dark you might find in a sewer or a bomb shelter when
the candles gutter out and you're left with nothing but fear
and the smell of death. It was more the darkness of an airline
cockpit, punctuated with countless blinking LEDs and the
electric hum of a thousand servers. Other rooms were lit like
the inside of an abattoir. Calling the basement where the code
breakers worked the Crypt had been somebody's idea of a joke,
a pun; unusually, it had stuck, perhaps because calling it the
Basement wouldn't work in a building where we all suspected
there were other floors below it, though none of us knew how
many or how to access all of them. There were doors where
by rights there wasn't any call for doors.

That afternoon, the Crypt's famously brutal air condition-
ing didn't feel much colder than the street outside. Warren
was wearing a sick-green fleece under his white lab coat, which
he generally did, although sometimes in summer it was a grey
V-neck pullover with a purple trim in the neck that looked like
it might once have been school uniform. Warren was a small
man. Not just short – although he was; I'm not especially tall
but I could comfortably have rested my chin on his head, had

the occasion ever arisen – but also small-boned, like a garden bird, his sloping shoulders no wider than any of the countless buff folders on his desk. Only his head was adult-sized, the forehead higher and balder than most, the chin small and pointed, giving him the appearance of a cartoon megalomaniac's captive mad scientist, or a miniature Roswell alien. He had been working at the Faculty longer than I had, longer than anybody could remember. The thick rubber soles of his shoes squeaked as he walked across the tiled floor to collect a single sheet from a printer, squeaked again as he returned to hand it to me.

*Sdhl asodi id asdschop wiojdslkjhdf sdoifj oifj sdfjo oisd oisdif iojsd f s dfs dfs d f sdfjs df sodjf o cvoljsdfmnouz chi cvoiew apoi.*

There was plenty more like that, but I didn't bother reading it.

I said, "I preferred his early work."

"He must have changed the book."

Book codes have been around about as long as books, Warren told me when I first brought him copies of Stephen's journal. They'd always been easy, if tedious, to decipher manually, provided you knew the source book. Digital scanning made the whole thing much simpler, and very, very quick. But you still had to know the book. At the time, a year or two earlier, we'd had several dead-ends before I alighted on *City of God*. With hindsight, I realized it should have been obvious from the start: Stephen's copy rarely left his bedroom desk, where it sat behind his typewriter, its pages interleaved with torn scraps of paper covered in tiny annotations and cross references. Mary had written her doctorate on Augustine. If Warren wondered why my then fifteen year-old son wrote his journal in code, or why I wanted it deciphered, he didn't ask; if I wondered why Warren apparently agreed, unofficially, without reporting me or passing on the product to his superiors, I didn't ask, either. I might have assumed that he'd known Mary, and was doing it more as a favour to her than to me.

When he said Stephen must have changed the book I didn't have to think too long. I said, "Try Marcus Aurelius. *Meditations*."

"Aurelius? You son's a real chip off the old block, isn't he?"

He didn't mean me. I wasn't the stuff from which my son had been fashioned.

He said, "Which edition?"

"Penguin classics."

"But which year?"

I said I'd have to get back to him. It would have to be at least fifteen years old, probably rather more.

I returned to my own office, by which I mean the space on the third floor that Simmons, Leach and I had colonized and in which Butler had more recently been installed. I offered to make them tea, or coffee, because that's what you did – if you didn't it would be noticed and remarked upon, especially by Leach, who rarely made tea himself – but I was lucky with the timing and no one took up the offer.

I sat down, deliberately scraping my right thigh along the metal edge of my desk. I unlocked the drawers, and from the second I withdrew a buff folder, identical to all the other buff folders on my desk, and on the desks of my colleagues, except that in this case the white adhesive label stuck over two or three previous labels said Exley: my own name, and that of my son. I skimmed the printed pages it contained. One, chosen at random and dated a few months earlier, contained a passage I had highlighted:

*Montaigne quotes Cicero that to philosophize is to learn how to die. He says life without the possibility of suicide would be insufferable. Camus says the only truly serious philosophical problem is suicide. Are they saying the same thing?*

To an observer – to Leach, perhaps, who was generally more interested in what was happening on other people's desks than on his own – it might have looked like I was working, albeit without any great urgency. My actions – reading a page of typescript, scribbling a note or two in the margin, pausing, thinking, perhaps making connections, joining the dots, drawing a pattern, clarifying the story of a crime, a confession, a conspiracy (although that would of course have been an inference on Leach's part, and not an observation) – my actions were identical to those of any man in sedentary, bureaucratic employment. And yet I was not working. I was not trying to determine if Simmons' crock of shit was in fact a crock of shit; I was not reviewing or making progress with any of my own caseload; I was reading the deciphered versions of my son's journal.

*No. Cicero – and Montaigne – wanted philosophy to educate us out of the fear of death – by encouraging us to live well while we are still alive. At heart, they were moralists. Camus asks us whether, having been born, we should continue to live at all.*

Nobody should be surprised when a fig tree brings forth figs. It was one of those things Mary used to say. I didn't mind. I just thought it was pretentious and possibly self-defeating to appeal to a second-century Roman emperor-slash-philosopher when pointing out the bleedin' obvious. Eventually, I'd said this aloud. Mary laughed and asked if I really thought she didn't know and hadn't said it anyway, to see how long it would take me to react? And I said of course I did, because otherwise I couldn't ever have married her, could I?

Nobody should be surprised when a teenager reads Camus and wonders why we don't all just kill ourselves. We had even had that conversation once, before he began his journal and we no longer had to. He asked if it was worth living and if so, why? I was pretty sure I'd had a similar conversation with Mary, a very long time ago, so instead of answering the question directly, I said, "Is it worth dying?" And when he said no, I said: "Then what choice do you have?"

It seemed to satisfy him; at any rate, he didn't ask again.

Now, in my office, not working, I read:

*Suicide is self-indulgent. Cheap. Easy. An abdication of our struggle, of our duty to make the world a better place.*

Oh, dear. Duty? A better place? The first time I'd read that passage, a month or so earlier, I'd been almost glad that Mary hadn't been there to read it. She would have been so proud. She might not have said I told you so, but she would have thought it: a chip off the old block, indeed. But in a year or two, he'd leave home. He would go away to university and stop writing his coded journal; in time, he would die. And the world would not be a better place.

I turned the page.

*What does it matter what I do? Or whether I do nothing at all?*

Doing nothing was the closest I'd ever come to an ambition. But unlike Stephen, I'd been around long enough not to take it literally.

Butler was standing by my desk, waiting. I had no idea how long she'd been there, or whether she'd been reading over my shoulder. Had she spoken? Had she asked a question to which she was expecting some reply? I quickly shuffled the pages of Stephen's journal back together and closed the folder. She had two empty cups in her hand. Gratefully, I said, "Yes, please."

She took the dirty, still tepid mug from my desk and went to make tea.

Leach yawned.

Simmons said, "Are we boring you?"

"Not you. Them." He flapped a hand towards the precarious pile of buff folders on his desk. "I'm pretty sure there was a time, when I was young, when suicide bombers weren't boring."

"When you were young?"

"It's a reasonable supposition."

Butler returned with the tea and we worked until it was time to leave.

WHAT DOES ANYBODY DO?

W HY SHOULDN'T WE be surprised? I asked
Stephen that evening.

I had stopped off on the way home from work to buy a
bag of figs, mainly as an excuse to re-open the discussion and
check the date on Stephen's - Mary's - paperback. I brought
them out after dinner and we sat at the table splitting the soft
skins with our nails and teeth, sucking at the flesh inside.
Stephen looked at me as if expecting a trick, or an unfunny
joke.

I ploughed on. "I mean, they're fig trees, I understand that.
But figs are still amazing."

This was desperate stuff. Philosophy was not my subject.
Also, the figs I'd bought were not amazing: they were barely
ripe, but had already turned brown inside. You couldn't get
decent figs any more than you could get decent avocados.

But Stephen took the bait. "Not really," he said. "If a fig-
tree produced an orange - or a plate of spaghetti, or a bicycle
- *that* would be amazing. A fig is just a fig."

I dropped a star-shaped fruit, split open but uneaten, onto
my plate. It landed with the soft plash of a dog's turd on
tarmac.

I said, "So why underline it?"

I expected him to say he hadn't, that he'd found the underlining there already when he opened it. Then I could say:
"Oh, really. Are there any other annotations?" I could ask him

to show me the book again, and – while skipping as lightly as possible over the dangerous topic of his mother – I could check the publication date and hand him back the book and we could watch the TV news. Instead he said, "I'd been thinking about Granddad." Which wasn't at all where I'd expected the conversation to go.

Stephen never knew my father – who died long before Stephen was born – and had met Mary's father only once, fifteen years earlier, when he was two.

"Your mother's father?"

"No, yours."

In my surprise, I said, "Why?" Which is one of those questions the Faculty always teaches its recruits to deploy with care. It might seem open – a question you can't answer with a simple yes or no, and so have to keep talking, keep incriminating yourself – but all too often it sounds like an accusation: subjects clam up. Two or three years earlier, when Stephen said he wanted to study philosophy, and I asked why, he'd shrugged. He said that Cicero thing he'd later written in his journal, about learning how to die. I laughed and said most of us seem to manage it without reading Greek. "Latin," he said, "and I don't suppose he meant it literally." Neither of us mentioned Mary, then. Now, he shrugged again.

I said, "You think I'm a fig?"

He shrugged again. He was seventeen, what did I expect?

He stood and carried his plate over to the sink, began to run hot water for the washing-up.

I said, "You think he worked for the Faculty, so I work for the Faculty?"

It wasn't a secret, my father's story, if you could call it that.

26

He'd been a watchman, a beacon keeper; he had committed suicide. It was something of an occupational hazard.

I said, "It's different."

Stephen took a wooden spoon and scraped the bottom of a saucepan. He said, "So what did he do?"

"He was a beacon keeper. You know that."

"I know. But what did he *do* – when he wasn't watching out for signals?"

"I don't know. Chopped firewood, mended the hut, read, argued with his partner, grew a few vegetables, maybe. What does anybody do?"

"You think they argued?"

"Two of them shut up together for months at a time? What do you think?"

Stephen stopped scraping the pot, but I could see there was still rice stuck where the bottom met the side of the pan. I thought: *we* don't argue, but then we mostly only meet at dinnertime.

"What did he think about?"

I laughed. My father had spent most of his adult life on the top of a mountain watching out for fire signals on surrounding hills. There must have been some reason, I suppose, but it probably wasn't the opportunity to contemplate the mysteries of the universe. If Stephen was hoping to find an hereditary explanation for his interest in philosophy, he'd have been better off looking to his mother, but I didn't say so. I thought, if Cicero was right, perhaps my father had been a philosopher after all: he'd certainly known how to die. But I didn't say that, either.

I said, "He kept a diary for a while."

"So you've said."

"You're welcome to read it, if we can find the thing. It's mostly about food, though."

That's how I remembered it. About a month after the funeral the Faculty had delivered a small package of my father's belongings – a change of clothes, a couple of slim, well-thumbed paperbacks, a hunting knife, a small black notebook – which my mother had posted on to me unopened. As far as I could remember, the diary mostly recorded what my father ate, and most of that was porridge and molasses. A few tinned sardines.

"Your grandfather wasn't much of a writer."

All the same, when we finished the washing up, rather than watching the news, Stephen suggested we take torches and climb up to the attic to search the boxes stored up there. I was surprised he was interested, and would have been happier to let the matter drop, but I couldn't think of any real reason to say no.

I'd never had much use for memorabilia. It was all there, though – faded remnants of my parents and Mary's parents, of Mary herself, and Stephen, their birth certificates and driving licenses and school reports and wedding invitations and rubber bands that would come apart, now, the moment you touched them, their threadbare toys and tarnished silver hip flasks, photographs of family holidays, of women and men who looked old at thirty wearing three-piece suits on the beach, scrapbooks full of recipes, fuel bills and title deeds and builders' guarantees, but only because it was easier to shove it up into the attic than cart it to the tip.

Look at this, though, Stephen would say, and this!

I hadn't wanted to be there – would rather have been watching the news, even if there was nothing in the news, even

28

if I'd spent another day making sure that there was nothing in the news – but I caught a little of his eagerness. There was a certain pleasure in mild peril as we stepped carefully from joist to joist for fear of crashing through the plaster ceiling into the bedrooms below; in blowing the dust from books to make each other sneeze; in the hunt for my father's diary which I nonetheless hoped we wouldn't find, and didn't.

We put everything back into the boxes, everything except the picture of Mary as a child that Stephen slipped into his pocket when he thought I wasn't watching. We tucked the cardboard flaps under and over each other and descended the ladder backwards, one at a time, with our torches between our teeth. On the landing we brushed the sooty cobwebs from our clothes.

Stephen said, "Thanks, anyway."

"Good night. Sleep well."

I went downstairs and tipped the fig skins and the untouched fruit back into the grocer's paper bag and dropped the bag into the bin. I made a pot of tea, but forgot to pour it. I listened for the patter of the typewriter, but for a long time the house was silent. When I went up to bed myself the light was still on in Stephen's room. As I passed his door I said good night again. "Don't stay up too late."

An hour later, though, it started. And in the days that followed, I heard the sound of Stephen typing more and more.

ItisdarkthereisnomoonnostarsCloudscovertheentireskymerge-withthehills Hecannottellthemapart

Theremusthavebeennightslikethatmanynightswhenitwas-notpossibletoseethe groundatyourfeetthetinmuginyour-handthesteamrisingfromthe ersatzcoffeethatpassedforcof-feetherewhentherewasnothingbecauseofcoursenothingwas the pointNothingbut the blacknessof the countrysideNot the fireon the nextmountainbecausefirewas the pointwhatthey-werelookingfor Iftherehadbeenanythingitwouldhavebeen the signalitwouldhavebeenwhytheywerethere Or morelikelywhy they werenottherebecause they mustsurelyhavedreamedhave-hopedaboveallnevertobeabletodo the onething they werethere-supposedlytodo the one thing they weretrainedfor if you couldcallittraining itcouldn'thavetakenlong Seethat? Seewhat? That? OhyesWhatisit? A signal That'sright a signal Whatdoy-oudonow? Isend the signal That'sright
     You'rein

Is itever thatdarkreally? Evenin the countryside? On a moun-tain? Eversodark you cannotmakeoutyourhand infrontof your facenomatterhowlong you stare, howlong you waittolet your eyesadapt to the lackoflight? Rarely,eventhen. When the cloud-scovered the moon and the stars and nootherlight shone on theirundersides, when no reflectedtrace of humanpresenceeilluminated the darkness of their present. The riverin the val-leywould not glisten, the brancheswould not be blackagainst the sky. On clearnights the smear of the MilkyWay, the sil-veriodidelandscape, the shimmer of leaves and the brilliance of the water.

The alarmhasrung. It is dark Mygrandfatherstands in the doorway a mugof coffeein his hand Jacobscalls to himto-close the door he wantsto read My grandfather wonders if Jacobsisgoing to read the scripthedgiven him thatmorning. He asks but Jacobsmerelysays again that he shouldclose the fuckingdoor, he wants the light on. My grandfather – Illcall him Eyquem It was nothisname it is not my name afterall – Eyquem knows Jacobs willnot read the script he'll read por-nography,if read is the word he'slookingfor. He will lookat-pictures and masturbate and if he Eyquem goesbackinto the huttoosoon the sweetalmondsmellofsemen willstill be in the air. He can'tblame Jacobs but he wishes he would read the script. There is lessthan a fortnightto go

He closes the door behindhim and

And what? Remember: I can't goon. I'll go on tomorrow. Tomorrow is a Philosophytest. Logicalanalysis. I'll neverget-fucking logicalanalysis. It's basicallymaths and there's a reason I'm not doingmaths.

# THREE

"WHY DID YOU even take it?" Leach asked, and I asked back: "Why not?"

Such are the manoeuvres by which the pretence of conversation is maintained.

For a moment, though, Leach looked startled, as if confronted by a concept he had never encountered. He said, "You shouldn't let her push you around. She's not the boss." Which was true, but hardly relevant. I had not been pushed around.

This conversation was also taking place in a pub – the same pub, of course, The Butcher's Arms – a week or so after the one about Stephen's unnatural habit of asking how my day had been when I got home, a little less than a week after Warren's algorithms had slowly, painfully adapted themselves to the switch from Augustine to Aurelius. He'd asked if I thought the change were merely alphabetical, if Stephen might be making his way along the bookshelf, which would be helpful, he said, albeit poor tradecraft on Stephen's part, as it might allow us to anticipate future changes in source; I said I thought there might be more to it than that. Checking the publication date while Stephen was in the shower, I had flipped through the book again and found another passage he, or Mary – probably Mary – had underlined. It came back to me now, sitting in the Butcher's watching Leach drink the beer I'd bought. *Begin your day by telling yourself: Today I shall be meeting with interference, ingratitude, insolence, disloyalty, ill-will and selfishness.* Mary had written it out on a five-by-four index card and taped it to the mirror in the bathroom, so we saw it first thing every morning. It was as if Aurelius had worked for the Faculty himself, she said.

It was still December, Christmas still a lurking threat, the weather outside still colder than a penguin's smile. Simmons had left. It was Nicola's birthday, herdaughterNicola, she'd explained. As if that were not a reason to spend as long in the pub as possible, Leach said, after she'd gone. Butler, as usual, had never arrived; so it was just me and Leach and all the other drinkers we didn't know cluttering up the place. It was unusually crowded for a Tuesday night, I thought. Christmas might be coming early.

"What difference does it make?" I said, realizing I'd dropped the conversational ball.

"It's a question of identity."

Really, he was full of surprises sometimes. I looked at my glass, which from any perspective was most definitely not half full. It was Leach's round.

"Not identity," he said. "Self-esteem." Which, to be fair, was not something he was short of.

I looked up, looked – as I tried so hard to avoid doing most of the time – above his loosened tie and grubby shirt-collar, looked into his face, into his eyes, and saw a moment of panic before he rocked back in his chair, laughed like he was coughing up phlegm, and said, "Okay, okay, I'll get the beer."

He rose, trying to reach the bar the hard way, squeezing between two young women dressed in inexpensive business suits – knee-length skirts and waisted jackets – that would have been identical had one of them not been grey, the other navy blue. I wondered, really, what difference it made, taking

Simmons' case. I had spoken without thought, instinctively –
it was a conversation, or a variant on a conversation we'd had
many times – and I knew I was right. There were only so many
hours in a day. The time I spent on Simmons case was time I
would not spend working on another. It would make no difference to me – or to the backlog piled up in our in-trays and
trickling constantly through the Faculty's internal post. There
was no shortage of work, and no prospect that we would ever
run out of things to do. There was enough stupidity on all
sides to be sure of that. Lives might be saved – that is, deaths
postponed – or might simply be swapped for other lives, one
plot thwarted, another allowed to proceed, a shooting spree
substituted for a suicide bomb, a train derailment for a poisoning of the water supply. Or, more likely, one crock of shit for
another, with no one any closer to their death than we all were
from the simple, inexorable passage of another working day.

Leach, with greater care and more florid apologies than
were strictly necessary, was easing his way back between the
young women whose conversation he had previously interrupted, carrying two fresh pints. It was a constant source
of surprise that the beer in the Butcher's was actually not
bad.

He had been right about one thing: Simmons wasn't
our boss. Not yet, at any rate. Of the four of us she seemed
much the most likely candidate for promotion. Butler was
too new, Leach too lazy, while I had no ambition and had, I
hoped, done nothing to attract the attention of the fifth floor.
Simmons was at least competent.

The more interesting, or at any rate the more debatable,
question was whether there was a vacancy to be promoted
into. We had not seen Gibbon for some months, but that

was not unprecedented. Communication between floors at the Faculty was mostly conducted by memorandum: occasionally, in extremis, by telephone. Once in a while, however, Gibbon would appear. He would make small talk. He would remind us – through an habitual smile and yellowed teeth – that our work, although it could never be celebrated, was of the highest importance, that there was no limit to what we could achieve, provided we were able to forgo the credit. He would insert his thumbs into his armpits while he spoke, then tug his waistcoat tight over his protuberant belly. He would march off, leaving us to return to our anonymous heroism, buoyed up by the spirit of common endeavour. It was a speech he must have inherited, because it was identical in all its platitudes to that of his predecessor, who had appointed each of us, including Gibbon himself (but not Butler, who was too recent a recruit). It is possible the speech was included somewhere in the Faculty's protocols; perhaps even in the Divisional Director's job description. But we had not heard it now for several weeks.

Gibbon hadn't said he was taking leave; his wife had not rung to say that he was ill. But, shortly after he was last seen on our floor, the flow of memoranda and new cases had abruptly ceased. Perhaps there had been a sudden, unreported cessation of hostilities? It seemed unlikely. A fortnight or so later, the memoranda – but no calls – began to trickle through again. Still, none of us had seen him. There had been no pep talks, no awkward conversations about sport.

Leach said flatly, "Cheers."

I emptied my first glass, moved onto the new one he had brought me.

He gestured back towards the bar. "Would you?"

I shook my head, objecting to the question more than answering it. But the fact was that I wouldn't, for a variety of reasons, only one of which was Mary.

Leach held up his hands, palms outward. "If we can't talk about work . . ."

"Or politics . . ."

"Or current affairs."

"Literature."

"Philosophy."

"Or soaps . . ."

"What else is there?"

There was a beat. It was another old routine. But this time Leach added, "Seriously, though. Why?"

"Seriously?"

"Why do we do it?"

"Why not?"

"Because it's all so fucking boring."

This, perhaps surprisingly, was not an old routine. "You sound like Stephen. My son, Stephen."

"I know who Stephen is."

"He's seventeen."

"I know. You mention it a lot. Did you know that?"

I sighed. I did know. It was a pattern and I had recognized it. I wondered what Stephen was doing at that moment. Homework, possibly. Tattooing the name of a girl on the inside of his wrist with a leaky biro, perhaps, although that seemed less likely. There was a girl, sometimes, in his journal, but even there she was never named. More likely he would be preparing supper. I hoped he'd use the chops I'd bought at the weekend, before they went off.

"You say 'boring' like it's a bad thing."

I only said it because our pints were still nearly full and the conversation had to go somewhere. I didn't want a conversation with a truculent teenager, even one who was grown up. The great blessing of Stephen's journal – the reason he wrote it in the first place – was precisely that we didn't have to discuss this stuff. So why would I with Leach?

I said, "Humans are the only animals bothered by monotony." It was another thing Mary used to say.

"We're the only ones bothered by suicide bombers, too," Leach said. "So what?"

I glanced instinctively around the pub – but, honestly, what could be more unremarkable, more innocent, than two men discussing terrorism after a hard day's work?

I said, "The two may be connected."

"Everything's connected."

There it was: the credo of the Faculty. It ran through everything we did – through every statistical analysis, every surveillance operation, every raid, every interrogation – the way misery and pain run through history; except, in this case, it's bollocks.

I said, "No it isn't."

"Well, it's just waiting for us to make the connections. Isn't that what Gibbon always says?"

"He does, but he's wrong."

I didn't want to get diverted into whether what Gibbon always said should now be in the past tense. I said, "Mostly everything's just random data."

"In which we recognize patterns."

"From which we make up stories . . ."

"Which make sense of the chaos."

"It's still chaos."

Leach shrugged and swirled the beer in his glass. "But it's *our* chaos."

"Exactly," I said. "They're *our* stories. We make them up. They don't change anything but us."

Leach said, "So what? Now who's talking like a teenager?"

It was the lust for endings, for significance. Stories end: *that's* how they make sense. But even if the world-historical tedium of our age was connected to the willingness to blow ourselves – and each other – to smithereens, it still didn't mean anything. From a broader view, a view that refuses to join the dots, nothing ever ends, or even stops.

I said, "You're only bored because you expect things to change all the time."

"What's wrong with that?"

What was wrong with that? I wanted nothing more than that nothing ever happen; feared above all that nothing should ever change. It was the human dilemma, I supposed: horror either way.

"You think things should lead somewhere."

"Maybe."

"But they don't. Boredom is the consciousness of time passing without progress."

Leach eyed me warily.

"It is indistinguishable from bliss."

*Bliss?* Where on earth had that come from?

Mary. That's where it had come from. Her thesis on St Augustine, I shouldn't wonder.

It was not the sort of thing to say to Leach. He checked his watch and swallowed most of his remaining beer.

He said, "It's time I got my train."

When I got home, there was a fire in the grate and Stephen was grilling chops. I asked if they were still all right, the chops; he said they were. He'd boiled and mashed the last of the potatoes, and braised a cabbage with caraway seeds.

He asked how my day had been, and I said it had been all right. That surprised him.

"All right?"

Not all right, I thought. Intolerable. Tolerable. What difference did it make? I had tolerated it.

I thought of Leach. I said, "Not really. Boring."

"How boring?"

"Spectacularly boring."

He laughed. He stirred the cabbage. "Isn't that an oxymoron?"

Was it? I wasn't sure.

I said, "What have you been up to? Apart from cooking?"

After a sarcastic pause, he said, "Going to school."

"But after that?"

"After that I wrote an essay."

"Oh, yes? What about?"

"Stuff."

I breathed deeply. I closed my eyes. If I asked what stuff, he'd ask if I really wanted to know, and we both knew the honest answer would be: not really. It was just the debt I owed for having brought him into the world. I opened my eyes.

"What sort of stuff?"

He looked at me askance and said, "Homer's repetition of stock phrases and the oral tradition."

"Right."

He said, "Dinner's ready."

He put the food on the plates and carried them over to the

table. I poured myself a glass of wine from a bottle I'd opened at the weekend. I wondered if I should offer Stephen one. No: he was seventeen. On the other hand: he was seventeen. I poured us both water. I thanked him for the food, which, for a while, we ate in silence.

"It happened again, while I was working."

He meant the knocking on the wall. I said, "Next door?"

He nodded.

"The same?"

I had never heard it.

He said, "It's never the same. By the law of averages I suppose he must repeat himself. But I can't spot it."

We both sawed at our chops in silence.

I said, "Did Homer repeat himself a lot?"

"Dad."

"What?"

He sighed. "The dawn is always rosy-fingered. Ships are "hollow", "black" or "beaked". He called the sea "wine-dark" about a zillion times."

"Which is odd . . ."

"Dad, if you say "it's all Greek to me" again, I'll stab you with this fork, okay?"

"It's just . . ."

He switched the fork to his right hand, curling his fist around it, ready.

". . . wine's red," I said. "Or white. It's nothing like the sea."

After dinner we watched the news. A ceasefire had broken down, a bomb exploded in a marketplace. An industry had collapsed; a new train line would be built. A minister had resigned for personal reasons. The lottery jackpot had not been claimed, and would be rolled over for the seventh time. In local news . . . something unpleasant had happened, then something good, but the words were drifting past, depositing no meaning.

Tomorrow's weather would be cold. Snow was possible, but not likely, except on high ground.

Stephen yawned.

I said it was probably time he went to bed.

A few minutes later I heard the muffled thwack of type-writer keys striking paper, the faint ping of the bell as he reached the end of a line and swept the carriage return from left to right.

Stephen's growing interest in his grandfather – or in whatever version of his grandfather he was inventing – might not be the healthiest obsession for a moody, Camus-reading teenager. But a young man who came home from school, lit the fires, wrote an essay on Homer, and cooked pork chops and cabbage for dinner wasn't going to come to too much harm, was he? No more than the rest of us, anyway.

L OGICALANALYSIS IS GETTINGEASIER. For now. OldGoatfucker probablystill has something up his sleeve. But we got last week's test back today. I got anA.

Shewaswearing the greenskirt and the patternedtightsto-day. I walkedpast her atlunchtime. She was standing with her friends. I couldhavesworn she winkedatme, if I didn'tknow that wasn'tpossible.

Is it possible?

So she commands, full of her high hopes.

and leans against it. He can see nothing, hear nothing. It is perfect, he thinks. Some shrieking bird or copulating fox way, way down the mountain will no doubtspoil it soon. No, not spoil it. A little death and sex will onlyintensify the silence.

Eyquempushes himselfgently away from the door. He steps carefully along the path he knows, without needing to see it. He feels weightless, suspended, which is why he comes out alone on nights like this whenever there is no light. It clears the mind.

In less than two weeks they'll be here. Brooks from the north and Cable from the west. It will be Christmas; they will be four. It's his turn to choose what they will do, how they will celebrate the holiday. He has decided; he has given Jacobs the script that, so far, Jacobs has not read. Brooks and Cable will have to read their parts overnight. That will be all right, though; their parts are small. They'll be in dustbins all the time and can keep their scripts with them, out of sight. It might work.

It has to work. This is his choice and he may not get another chance for years.

He has met Brooks before, six years ago, at Brook's choice. They played Monopoly. Eyquem was the little dog, Brooks the top hat. He was large, flabby, and red-faced. A top hat – and perhaps an embroidered waistcoat and a monocle – would have suited him. In a nightcap and pyjamas, Eyquem thinks, he'll be perfect for the part. Neither of them had won at Monopoly. It had been the man from Brooks' north, the smoothing iron – Eyquem can't remember his name – who bought the stations and the green streets and then the dark blue ones, the most expensive on the board, and that was that. A good game, though. It had lasted hours. It was so much more fun, Brooks said, than playing with only two.

He's never met Cable, who might be new, but equally might not. It was always possible that whenever he visited the beacon to the west, Cable himself had been visiting elsewhere. If Cable had visited Eyquem's beacon before, he might have been away himself – playing Monopoly with Brooks, perhaps. There were two watchmen for each beacon: at Christmas and midsummer one stayed behind, while the other visited an immediate neighbour from an adjacent point to the north, south, east or west. Or both watchmen stayed to host two visitors. The Faculty's timetabling was complex, like a human version of the game of Go. There must be some beacons – those on the coast – with only three neighbours, which would reduce the options and complicate the arithmetic. He and Cable could have worked on adjacent mountains for twenty years without ever crossing paths. Now, as the rotas shift, they might meet three times in the next five years. They might become friends. For the moment, however, he is more concerned about the play, about whether Cable will be up to it. Luckily, his isn't much of a part. Things have worked out rather well, in fact. Cable is the least of his problems.

Eyquem believes he has been walking in a straight line. He is no longer following the path, which takes a spiral route around the mountaintop, like the lengths of apple peel that Jacobs tries to cut with his hunting knife. He has been proceeding consistently downhill, each footfall lower than the last, his body lightly braced against gravity, a few degrees off the perpendicular. He knows, from habit and because he can visualize the geometry as clearly as if there were light, as if he were studying a childhood textbook on a worn and ink-stained desk in front of him, that if he turns ninety degrees – whether right or left makes no difference – and maintains a consistent altitude, by placing his right foot just a fraction higher than his left food with each step (if he has turned to the right) or his left foot just a fraction higher than his right (if he has turned to the left) for as long as it pleases him to do so – for as long, perhaps, as it takes him to work out the play's staging in his mind, to block out the moves in his head – then he will circumscribe the cone of the mountain. And when the time comes, when he is tired or has completed his mental preparation, he can at any point simply turn ninety degrees to the right (if he has turned right the first time) or to the left (if he has previously turned left) and walk consistently uphill, each step higher than the last, to find the hut again. There is no need to return to the precise point at which he first turned – which, in the dark, of course, he could never recognize. Trees are a problem, and ditches, if he walks too far downhill before turning. He has banged his nose and wet his boots more than once. They spoil the purity of the section of the cone, at least in his mind. But he can't lose his way for long. The way back is always up. As long as he keeps placing one foot higher than the last he will eventually return, just as an Antarctic explorer has only to keep moving south eventually to reach the pole: the hut sits at the very highest point of the mountain, from which its beacon, if it were ever lit, could be seen from all sides.

On summer nights the hut is picked out by horizontal sunbeams long after the valleys are enclosed in darkness. The summer solstice shows can be performed outdoors, without torches. He wonders if it might have been better to wait until June. But in June it would not be his choice, and he had no idea when the rota would work round to him again. All the same, a summer performance might be better. Jacobs has to look out of the windows and describe what he can see: in December, all four of them would know that he could see nothing. But wasn't that the point?

He turns – to the right, tonight – and begins a clockwise course. The ground beneath his feet is firm – rock, or frozen earth. He has everything he needs, he thinks, except a wheelchair. A chair with wheels, to be more precise. He must empty the bins before Brooks and Cable arrive. He has chairs, and wheels – the wheels from the bicycle for the back, the casters from the battered three-seat chesterfield for the front. He wonders briefly how the chesterfield had ever been brought up here, to the top of a mountain, but that is not his problem. Perhaps it had been a prank? His problem is how he will attach the wheels securely to one of the wooden chairs.

Or would Jacobs be strong enough to push him around in the chesterfield itself?

He decides this is a problem he can put aside to solve another day, another night, as he has previously reserved the problem of lighting to be solved today. In his mind, he has conceived the production taking place outside, which would give them enough room to move – those who moved. Jacobs, in particular. It would also present their performance to the world, even if the world were not watching. But what if Christmas Eve were as dark as tonight? If there were no moon? They could each hold a paraffin lamp, he thinks, although Jacobs would need to put his down from time to time. That would be atmospheric, but would it work? Might their lamps be mistaken for the beacon? It seemed unlikely, but it was a risk. It was against the rules. Could the rules be bent for Christmas? Hardly, or they would not be rules. And what if it were snowing? They could perform indoors, inside the hut, but there would be very little space and he would have to work out all over again the blocking movements he had been through in his head. It would not be impossible, but it would not be ideal.

Ideal? There's a word he hasn't used for a while.

He pauses, bringing his feet together. He sniffs the air, but smells nothing. They are too high up here. The only scents he can imagine are those of cooking, or Jacobs' flatulence, which tend to be concentrated indoors. Or the intense odour of the beacon burning, which of course he has never experienced. If the beacon were burning, they'd probably have other things on their minds; but, all the same, he imagines it would smell strongly of pitch.

He steps on, right foot landing parallel to, but a little higher than, the left. He realizes with a distant sense of excitement, of scenting a kill, that the two problems he has been mulling over are connected after all. If Jacobs were strong enough to push him around on the chesterfield, with its casters, there'd be no need to dismantle it and the bicycle, or to find a way to attach the wheels to a wooden chair. Now he thinks about it, dismantling the bicycle is probably against the rules, too, even in the cause of art. It would also be more authentic. The script specifies an armchair on casters. He doesn't have an armchair as such, but the chesterfield is a closer match. It is conceivable that Jacobs could push him around in it, at least on the hut's wooden floor, the surface of which has been worn smooth, almost polished, over the years. But he couldn't possibly manage on the rough and rocky terrain of the mountaintop itself. If, unlike tonight, there were a moon, and stars, and the blurred proscenium arch of the Milky Way, they might perform outdoors and the chesterfield would not suffice; if there were no moon, or if it were snowing, they would have to remain inside, and it would. If Jacobs is strong enough.

He will have to wait and see. To keep a weather eye on the weather. To be prepared, either way, but not commit himself.

It is not a solution, as such, but obviates the possibility of a solution, for now. Which is enough.

He pauses again, both feet together. At least there'd be no audience to accommodate. That would be a real problem.

Satisfied, resolved, Eyquem turns ninety degrees to his left and steps briskly uphill. His foot lands much lower than it had started out and, in shock, he tumbles to his knees and then, gravity taking its toll, onto his head. He pitches over and over, gathering momentum, hurtling and bouncing down the mountain like a loose cartwheel, until collision with a tree root launches him into the air and he lands, flat on his back, face to the stars, if only there had been stars, with his head lower than his feet, just inches short of a bog hole that might have broken his neck, or drowned him at the very least.

M Y LEGS ITCHED: my thighs, and particularly my hips. The cold weather was to blame. It dried my skin, leaving irritated patches that looked like ringworm. On the train that morning, as I got hotter and began to sweat, I had tried to scratch my legs through the trousers of my heavy winter suit. The woman in front of me shrank away, but the carriage was too crowded to move far. I said nothing, and avoided her eye. Standard operating procedure for public transport. At the terminus, the doors opened and the crowd shifted and relaxed in the familiar peristaltic motion of disembarkation. The woman said – aloud, but to no one in particular – that some people should be locked up for their own good.

In the office, at my desk, I could scratch. Faculty desks – on the third floor, anyway – were made of olive-coloured metal, as if requisitioned from some military installation (which they may have been). They clanged and rattled if you dropped a pen or put a teacup down too heavily. The front edges were folded over, and, by rolling my chair back and forth, I could abrade my thighs and achieve some measure of relief, at the cost of occasionally tearing holes in my trousers. My colleagues would notice, of course. But they were used to it.

There might be plastic explosives.

It was possible. But it was far more likely that there weren't. There were still more addresses in the city that did not contain explosives than those which did. But that was little comfort: there were also more addresses that *did* contain explosives than would ever cross my desk. I had ordered surveillance, less by way of making a decision than of avoiding one.

Now, a week later, I had the report, which was predictably inconclusive. A man not known to the Faculty (large, forties, overweight, possibly Semitic, with a black beard and round, horn-rimmed spectacles) had left the flat at some point each morning (the times catalogued in an annex to the report now on my desk) and returned most evenings. On some days he had returned in the afternoon and gone out again; on others he had not. The report author concluded that the subject's movements were not consistent with those of a person in gainful employment. A woman, also unknown (Caucasian, late thirties, short, dyed-blonde hair) had also left and entered the flat on numerous but not predictable occasions. On Day 4, Sunday 15th December, at 16:07, the woman had been observed leaving the flat wearing slippers beneath a powder-blue raincoat; she had not returned until the following afternoon at 13:42. Other visitors, predominantly male (detailed in Annex C; no known targets) had arrived and departed at various times.

A crock of shit.

Perhaps.

Butler asked if I wanted coffee; Leach said he did. Butler said she wasn't asking him.

"But you will," he said.

"Ask you?"

Leach pushed his chair back from his desk, leant across and put his arm around Butler's waist. "Make me coffee, Butler."

"Make it yourself, pig."

Simmons did not look up from her desk.

More interesting than the report itself was the fact that Simmons hadn't asked me about it. Since passing over the case, in fact, she hadn't mentioned it at all. Which could mean one of two things. Either it was of genuinely no importance to her, and she'd simply been trying to ease her own impossible workload; or the case – and the way I handled it – was so important to her that she didn't want to draw attention to it by asking questions. By *not asking*, of course, she had now paradoxically drawn my attention to her feigned lack of interest.

Unless she really didn't care.

Which was it?

Butler returned with a tray of coffees. She left mine until last, until she could be sure that neither Leach nor Simmons was watching. As she put my cup beside the file on my desk, she discreetly placed beside it a tube of moisturising cream. She returned to her own desk without a word.

What was happening in that flat? A couple going about their business. Working, not working. Drinking, eating, making love, arguing, masturbating, seeing friends, and manufacturing explosives? The file said the man's name might be Volorik; he might be a journalist. Or a gambler. Or an arms dealer. He could be all three, I thought, but it was just as likely he was something else entirely. The data in the case was patchy, the sources partial and unreliable. The scenario was laughable and paranoid, like something you might hear on a late night radio call-in.

None of which meant it wasn't true. Or true enough.

I took a notepad from the drawer and laid it sideways on the desk in front of me. In the centre of a blank page I drew a circle. I scribbled it out, flipped the page and drew a diamond.

Inside the diamond I wrote: *Crock of shit?* From each side I drew an arrow leading to a box. Above the right hand arrow I wrote, *Yes,* above the left-hand arrow, *No.* In the *Yes* box I wrote: *Random?*

That was another question. Which meant a decision. It should be in a diamond. I was bound to get the logic wrong. Mary used to say that logic was the intersection of maths and philosophy, which might explain why Stephen didn't like it, and why I had no chance. I'd done Biology.

I scratched my leg, then the other leg.

The case was either nonsense or it wasn't. Even if were, it might still be genuine nonsense – the sort of false positive you can't avoid when you combine so much data, the way the Ancients stared at the stars until they couldn't help spotting animals and giants and fish. Or it could be another sort of nonsense, a pattern lightly sketched between the dots that made no more sense than Pisces, but had been deliberately concocted for a reader – Simmons or me – to find. Which would be a wholly different kettle of . . .

My mind was wandering. On the notepad I found I had drawn the simple outline of a fish, like the ones you see on windows or car bumpers. I carefully placed a dot for an eye, a downward crescent for a mouth, then scratched a jagged line through the whole thing. Concentrate, Exley.

If the case was a deliberate fiction, was Simmons the intended audience, or its author? Was she being set up, or was I?

Was the point to discredit one of us? Or to distract us from something else, something real?

Or both?

If Simmons' disinterest was feigned, she must have known the case was nonsense and, by passing it on, was deliberately dumping me in trouble. Or testing me. But, if it were genuine, she had just dodged a bullet.

Which was it?

I sipped the coffee Butler had made. It was milky and sweet. I drink my coffee black, no sugar. We are an intelligence service: she should have known that.

It was always possible the case was not a crock of shit at all, that there was a real plan to detonate real explosives and kill real people. Even then, it might still mean nothing much at all – except to the people killed, of course. Or their families. A real bomb could be the work of an isolated individual, a lone assassin, so to speak, on a frolic of his own.

There was one final option, the least plausible, the least statistically probable of them all: that the alleged plan was both real and part of a wider, organized and orchestrated terror plot of precisely the sort I was employed to detect and thwart. That it was, in fact, the reason I was here.

I took another sip of the sickly, beige liquid polluting my mug.

So: six possible scenarios. I ripped out the page I'd been drawing on and screwed it up. (Later I would flatten it out again. There were no litterbins in the Faculty, where everything had to be filed or shredded.) On a new page I wrote:

1) A genuine, 24-carat crock of shit
2) A fake plot, designed by parties unknown, for reasons unknown, to discredit Simmons
3) A fake plot, designed by Simmons, for reasons unknown, but possibly related to promotion opportunities, to discredit me
4) A fake plot, designed by Simmons and/or parties

unknown to divert the resources of the Faculty (including me) from some more significant plot or threat

5) A genuine, but isolated threat
6) A genuine, organized 24-carat terror plot

The question now was not which of these was right, or at least most closely resembled the reality I was dealing with. There was no way of knowing that yet, and the surveillance report added nothing. No, the question was, given these six possibilities, what should I do?

I went to lunch.

Before leaving the building, I decided to keep going down to the Crypt. Even if it were lunchtime, Warren would be there.

"I meant to say yesterday: congratulations."

He handed me a double-sided printed page; I gave him two new pages of typed numerals in return.

"What have I done?"

"Not you. Stephen. Another A."

It took me a while to remember that Stephen's journal had anticipated a logic test. He had not mentioned it to me and we had not, of course, discussed it – how could we? Meanwhile, Warren's interest in Stephen's progress was becoming alarmingly avuncular.

I found it hard to call Warren Warren. I had to assume it was his surname, because that's what he was called in the Faculty, but it *could* have been a given name. It could even have been both: there are parents that cruel. And in a world where, if a colleague kindly, quietly, wordlessly, gave one a tube of moisturiser to relieve the incessant itching in one's legs, it was nonetheless unthinkable to address that colleague as Brigid, the prospect of accidentally calling the cryptologist by his first name, of appearing to express familiarity, to attempt intimacy, even, would paralyse my tongue. I found myself incapable of addressing him as anything at all, and avoided doing so. But still he seemed to think he could talk to me about my son, just because he was doing me a favour.

Stephen's journal had more than once mentioned a girl in his Greek and English classes, but had never named her. When Warren enquired how the romance was progressing, I always pointed out that we could not infer from the evidence available that 'X' and 'she' referred to the same girl each time, or that there was any romantic interest involved.

"You haven't asked him?"

"Of course I haven't asked him."

After a pause, he would straighten the edges of the pages he was handing over, and say: "No, I suppose not."

From time to time, however – mostly when the journal touched on suicide – concern would get the better of his discretion. He would tell me that I *must* talk to Stephen, that I must let Stephen talk to me.

"Really, Exley," he would say. "Silence is a killer. Suicide is the most common cause of death among young men."

"You know that's more to do with antibiotics than emotional constipation."

"What?"

"They're too healthy to die of anything else."

Still, I felt obliged to read Stephen's journal, although I would have preferred not to. He knew – broadly – what I did for a living. He knew that encrypting it would attract my attention without hindering my ability to read it. I had to assume that he *intended* me to read it, that I was the audience he had in mind as he sat, each evening, after finishing his homework, tapping away at his mother's typewriter, rattling the carriage and ringing the bell with no attempt at concealment. At the same time, he would know we couldn't discuss what I'd read, because that would be to acknowledge that I'd read it. I had to assume that's why he wrote it in the first place.

Stephen was not responsible for the misfortune of his own birth. That was my doing – Mary's and mine. Awareness of his life, if not actual interest in it, was the least – and the most – I could do in the circumstances. I looked forward to the time, less than two years away, when he'd leave home for university.

I said, "An A, yes. He's a clever boy. He'll be fine."

"What would you like?"

I was standing at the counter. I hadn't noticed the queue in front of me shuffle forward. A huge steel urn squatted on the counter hissing steam in sympathy with the waitress. I'd been trying to demonstrate to myself that it was possible for mind to outwit matter, to prove that I could choose not to feel physical discomfort. Distraction as a form of distraction, if you will. My legs might itch, but could I out-think the sensation? And, if I did, was the itch still there? Cogito ergo non . . . whatever the Latin for itch might be. Mary would have known. I would not scratch.

"Are you eating?"

"Sorry. I was miles away."

I scratched my leg.

The menu board on the wall behind the counter offered a dozen permutations of all-day breakfast, plus meat and three veg.

I could cultivate the faculty of indifference.

"Hello? Last chance."

"Baconandmushroomsandwich. Please."

"Bacon?"

"And mushroom."

"Anything else?"

I shook my head. "No, thanks. Tea. Please. No sugar."

I paid and took a seat. Another waitress, not the one at the counter, came and cleared away the dirty plates. She sprayed the plastic table and wiped it with a damp cloth, smearing ketchup and grease towards the edges where they might have a better chance of staining my suit. I sat back to give her room. The pain in my backside – more than an itch – returned. The waitress brought a mug and placed it in front of me, the teabag still bleeding into the brick-coloured milky liquid.

"Sugar's there."

It was Mary who told me about the faculty of indifference. When she was young and still new to the job, not long after she'd completed her PhD, she tried to explain how philosophy might help in our career.

"Take Cioran," she said.

I think she was drunk at the time.

"Who?"

"He said as soon as a man loses the faculty of indifference he becomes a potential murderer."

We'd certainly been in a pub, I remember that. It might even have been the Butcher's Arms.

"Don't you find that suggestive? In our line of work?"

She said she liked to think that was why the Faculty was

called the Faculty, though she knew it wasn't.

I said it was hardly news that terrorists tend to be passionate about something or other, even if it was only their own martyrdom. She said it was more than that. The slightest deviation from indifference, she said, the smallest flicker of interest is a compromise that shatters the bonds of common humanity. You're free to torture and kill without compunction.

"Interest in what?"

"In anything."

"Like whether you're going to buy me another pint?"

"That would do it."

"But you are, aren't you?"

When she'd bought the round, she said most people never thought of indifference as a faculty. They assumed it was a given, like having brown eyes, about which there was nothing to be said worth saying. But really, she said, it's something you have to cultivate. It takes work.

"Isn't that an oxymoron?"

"Big word."

"I read too, you know."

"So what does it mean?"

"How can you cultivate indifference without caring whether you're indifferent?"

"The truly indifferent wouldn't care whether they cared or not."

There was something askew in that. Cultivating indifference to the quality of one's own indifference could easily lead a person to become paralysed by spiralling doubt, incapable of even the simplest, least significant decision – of ordering lunch, for instance. It could make life impossible. All the same,

I could see it might be something to aspire to. Recognizing the supreme unimportance of any decision or action I might take, or not take, could make it tolerable to live at all.

"Ketchup or brown sauce?"

Returning to the office, I noticed that the wind had dropped, but clouds had gathered over the city. They were black, dense, bearing snow like a sow heavy with its litter.

"Jacobs?"

"What?"

"I'm waiting."

"That's nothing new."

Eyquem is seated on the old chesterfield, which they have wheeled to the exact centre of the hut, to a point where two lines drawn through each pair of facing windows would have intersected. It is noon, still light, though only just. Still, the chesterfield and therefore Eyquem are facing south. He could have seen clear to the mountains, were it not for the dark glasses, and the handkerchief draped over his face. The handkerchief appears to be stained with blood. (In reality it is stained with tomato sauce from the last tin of pilchards.)

"But we've started. You have the first words. We'll work out the business later. You're supposed to say it's finished."

"I'm supposed to start by saying it's finished?"

Eyquem reaches up and pulls the handkerchief from his face.

"Haven't you read the script?"

"I thought it might spoil the story."

Jacobs is behind Eyquem, sitting on the table, which they have moved back against the north wall, under the window, to make room for the chesterfield. He is a large, flabby man at heart, although he has become inevitably smaller and leaner over the years. His flesh hangs in lugubrious folds from the underside of his face and arms and around his arse, like the stone robes of tragic statuary. Eyquem has not yet asked him to wheel the chesterfield with him in it.

"We'll try a read-through."

The table is deal, plain and rough. It is possible to imagine it having been regularly scrubbed smooth; now it is scarred and stained. Jacobs slides uncomfortably to his feet, sighing for effect. "I'll get my script." He walks a few steps over to the bed, the positioning of which had been the cause of a long-running dispute. From the start, both men agreed the bed should be placed against the east wall, opposite the door. But where, exactly? Eyquem favoured a central position, under the window. That way, when he woke in the morning, he could look out at the dawn; or, when he woke in the evening, he could watch the light die. Jacobs asked why on earth he'd want to do either. He asked it angrily, not as if he wanted to know the answer. He said they spent half their lives, twelve hours at a fucking stretch, looking out the fucking windows and he wasn't going to do it on his own fucking time. Jacobs wanted the bed right up against the northeast corner, away from the window. This was cosier, he said. He could pin pictures to the walls, and see *those* when he woke up, or went to sleep. The pictures he preferred were mostly of women, or knives. The women had few, if any, clothes and the knives had tooled blades and handles carved from single pieces of ram's horn. The argument continued for many months. There were changes of season that lent force, Eyquem thought, to his point about watching the light, but which made no difference to Jacobs' intransigence. Each took advantage of the other's absence – fetching water from the stream to the south, defecating in the stream to the north or (best of all, because of the time it reliably took) making their periodic bicycle trip down the mountain for supplies – unilaterally to re-locate the bed, until eventually, as Eyquem had long said they would, they reached a compromise. Whichever of them fetched supplies foreswore the right to move the bed until more supplies were due. Eyquem christened their dispute the "war of six feet". Jacobs said they only had four between them – eight, if you included the bed. But six feet was the distance the bed had moved each time. Like Flanders, Eyquem said, but Jacobs had no idea what he was talking about.

The iron frame bed is currently in the corner. Jacobs lowers himself to his knees, and begins sorting through the pile of magazines beside it. The magazines are mostly old, creased and dog-eared; repeated fingering has taken the shine off their pages. Amongst the pile he finds a slim paperback. As he stands up again, the alarm clock on the windowsill begins to ring. Jacobs stuffs a finger between the hammer and the bell, then switches it off. He looks out of the window, sees nothing. He walks anti-clockwise around the hut, pausing to stare out of the north, west and south windows in turn, before returning to the east. He winds up the clock and re-sets the alarm for thirty minutes' time.

"Nothing."

He has seen nothing.

In fact he has seen everything. Eyquem could describe it all, with or without the dark glasses and the blood-stained handkerchief, having scanned the same view twenty-four times a day for twenty years: mountains, forests, streams, rivers, hills, a road and farms in the valleys to the south where the village lies; the purple-blue smudge on the western horizon Jacobs claims is the sea but Eyquem says cannot be, it is too far from here to the ocean; a clear evening sky washed by earlier rain to a delicate primrose yellow; a buzzard stretching its wings and leaning into the faint breeze as it floats effortlessly above the hut. What Jacobs would not have seen, and has not seen, on any of the four neighbouring mountaintops, is a fire, a beacon of seasoned wood and pitch stacked ten feet high exactly like their own, alight. He does not need to do anything. He will be free for the next half hour. He has been a little clumsy re-setting the alarm clock. It may be more like forty minutes.

He is free.

He says, "Nothing to be done."

Putting the handkerchief back over his dark glasses, Eyquem says: "Have we started again? It sounds like we've started."


I'm reading *To the Lighthouse*. I'm sure no one in my class has read Virginia Woolf, not even X, who has read everything.

# TWO

## A BAD DAY

T HIS WAS WHAT a bad day looked like.

A day when something happened. Two things, in fact.

When Stephen asked me how my day had been – which he would – I'd have a new standard against which to measure the magnitude of my lies.

The first of the two was my fault; or, at least, had happened at my instigation.

Early that morning – while I lay in bed listening to the sounds of Stephen doing whatever it is he does in the bathroom, thinking that it was time I got up too, the breakfast wouldn't make itself – somewhere else, somewhere in the east of the city, police and security service personnel had been battering down the door of a third-floor flat in a low-rise, between-the-wars block. (We're always between the wars, as Mary used to say, if you take a long enough view.) They – the uniforms and the plainclothes – would have pointed their guns at anyone inside the flat, yelling at them to get down on the floor and not to fucking move. I hoped they hadn't discharged their weapons, although it was always a possibility. Some of the Faculty's operatives, I knew, did not share my profound desire that nothing – or at any rate, as little as possible – should ever happen, and regarded operations like this as the perfect opportunity to make damn sure that something *did*. Whether or not their firearms were discharged, however, it was a safe bet there'd been a punch or two, a kick, a blow to the head with a blunt instrument, for the legitimate purpose of establishing the ground rules, of letting everybody know exactly who was in charge and who was not to move or open their fucking mouths unless they were specifically ordered to. It was safer that way. The occupants of the flat – a large, round-faced man with spectacles; a short, blonde woman in her slippers – would have had their hands tied behind their backs with plastic cuffs and rough cloth bags pulled over their heads, none too gently. They'd have been hauled to their feet and led down three flights of stairs – I had to hope they'd used the stairs and no one had jumped or been flung from a balcony – and pushed into an unmarked van to be brought in for processing. The flat would have been sealed, and guarded. Later that morning, while I stood on the platform at my local station wondering if the next train, and the one after that, would be too crowded for me to board, the flat would have been comprehensively photographed, dusted for fingerprints and scraped for DNA samples. Computers, typewriters, books and papers, money, clothes and bedding, packets of food and spices would all have been packaged, tagged and carted away for inspection and analysis. Cushions and mattresses would have been cut open, floorboards levered up with heavy crowbars, sheets of plasterboard punctured and ripped from partition walls and ceiling joists. The air would have filled with dust, with the residue of long-dead human skin, pet hair and coarse black city soot, with disturbed plaster and cement and asbestos fibre and possibly – just possibly – with ammonium nitrate. By lunchtime it would all have been over, at least for the casual observer: nothing to see but a single, genuine police constable and a tagliatelle sprawl of scene-of-crime tape warning neighbours and journalists not to enter.

The whole point was that nothing should ever happen. That, if anything, is what we were for. There is a ghastly cliché you will have heard whether or not you know anything about our business. I remember Gibbon, or maybe Gibbon's predecessor, standing with his thumbs hooked into his waistcoat, his tongue slapping out saliva against his yellow teeth, opining that the other fellow – he even pronounced it fellah – only had to be lucky once, while we had to be right every single time. Except we couldn't be right every time and sometimes shit happened – Gibbon didn't say that – and sometimes you even had to do shit yourself, which might be worse. I would always – instinctively, professionally, viscerally – prefer to do nothing than something. But in this case, in the context of this particular crock of shit, I had weighed the options available and had concluded, unwillingly and on balance, that it was better *this* happen than any of the alternatives.

I tried to talk about it in the pub, partly because it was on my mind and I wanted to see how Simmons might react – it was supposed to be her case, after all – but mainly to stop Leach talking about what Butler had done, or not done.

Because that was the second thing that had happened. The second reason today was such a bad day, the reason we were quieter than usual, except Leach, who talked more than ever and only made things worse. Which was to be expected. The reason Butler, who never came to the pub, had come to the pub. Which wasn't.

"It's not your fault," Leach told her, although we all knew it was.

I said, "Chances are there's nothing there."

"Not now there isn't," Leach said. "Not after . . ." He made a rumbling sound and mimed an explosion with his hands.

"Shut up," Simmons said.

Butler, who never drank, wiped her nose with the back of her hand and said she wanted another drink.

I said, "Not there. In the flat."

"No one cares about your poxy flat," said Leach.

Simmons told him to go and buy more beer.

Butler said, "I just . . . the children . . ."

I said, "There weren't any children. Just a man and a woman; and probably nothing else."

But she hadn't meant in the flat; I knew she hadn't. She'd meant the house. Because the other thing that had happened, the thing that made today a truly, horrendously, appallingly bad day, wasn't going away. Even if it wouldn't be in that night's news.

Somewhere else that morning – not in the city, but in a town just sixty miles north and definitely within our jurisdiction – a man and a woman in their late thirties, married and professionally-qualified – she in architecture, he in the law – rose early, leaving the au pair to get their twin girls – Helen and Christina – out of bed and ready for school. They drove a few miles into the surrounding countryside: genteel, undulating, sheep-infested farmland marked by ancient hedgerows and, to their educated eyes, the thousand year-old scars of mediaeval strip farming. On the outskirts of an attractive village that boasted both a pub and a newsagent's, they knocked at the substantial front door of a Queen Anne manor house. It was the home of a junior defence minister and his wife, vice-president of a global oil company, of their three children, and of the nanny who, when she heard the knock, had been packing sandwiches, chopped carrots, dried fruit and three small bottles of unsweetened lime-and-ginger flavoured water into three lunch bags. The minister's driver-cum-security guard opened the door, and the woman – successful architect and mother of two – shot him in the face without a word. In the kitchen, she told the children and the nanny not to move, not to make a sound – but never once said, "And then you won't get hurt". Her husband, the lawyer and father of twin girls, sought out and brought downstairs at gunpoint the politician and his wife. Between them they lined up the whole family – father, the defence minister, on the left; mother, oil executive, on the right; the three children ranged by age and height between them; the nanny next to the mother – and ordered them to kneel. In an uninflected monotone, swapping sentences back and forth between them, the couple denounced the legal, moral and philosophical outrages allegedly perpetrated by both the minister's government and the executive's corporation. They were, it seemed, responsible for the deaths of thousands, the impoverishment of millions and God's abandonment of the city of man. The woman took six knives from an oiled hard-wood block on the counter next to a restaurant-grade gas stove. The knives had blades of folded Japanese steel and came in a variety of shapes and sizes: short and full-bellied, broad and fish-shaped, long and serrated. She laid them out on the floor, one in front of each member of the family. They were to slit each other's throats, she said, starting with the nanny, out of courtesy: she was only an employee, and not herself to blame. The children would be next, the mother or the father last; it was up to them. The last to go should kill himself (or herself), or they – the woman and her husband – would do it for them, if that was what it took.

Which is what they did.

The mother slashed the nanny's throat, hacking through

the tendons to the bone, then killed her daughter, the middle child, who had always been her favourite; then she begged her husband to kill her. He killed the youngest child, too. The eldest child (he was the eldest, after all) killed his father, stabbing through his Adam's apple, then slipped on the marble tiles, which were awash with blood kept slick and fluid by the underfloor heating installed that autumn by contractors working for the murderer/architect's practice, which had been engaged by the now-murdered couple to undertake substantial but historically-sensitive renovation work to their three hundred year-old home. He lay prostrate until the murderer/architect slit his throat, too. Then, captured with impressive clarity by the recently-installed security cameras that, by accident or design – and given her qualifications, one had to presume design – would survive what happened next, the architect/murderer-wife and her lawyer/murderer-husband embraced, pulled the rip-cords on each other's suicide vests, and blew the house to smithereens.

So far, so routine.

Well, not routine, exactly, but certainly predictable, if not actually predicted. Which was closer to the real problem.

The couple was one of ours. By which I mean: known to the Faculty. Their joint, double-barrelled surname was clearly typed on the adhesive label of a file which that morning – and each morning for the previous three months – had sat on Butler's desk: read, but unremarked. Any architect commissioned to remodel the home of a defence minister and an oil executive had obviously been vetted – along with her colleagues and her family – but, having been cleared, would still be subject to on-going surveillance and risk assessment. Hence the file.

All of which made it a much worse day for Butler, I had to assume, across whose desk those risk assessments had passed, than for me, Simmons or Leach.

Leach said, "I blame Gibbon."

"Of course you do," Simmons said.

Of course he did. Gibbon wasn't there. Who else was he going to blame?

"Not just because he isn't here," Leach said. "But because . . . well, he isn't *here*."

"Right."

"He should have . . ."

Butler said, "I just . . ."

"Shh."

"Those children."

"Don't talk about it."

"You can't talk about it."

"Don't think about it."

I said, "Brigid?"

A silence fell around us.

Simmons said, "Stiff upper lip?"

I ignored her. "It's not your fault."

It was, though. Even if it was also Gibbon's fault.

When I left, Butler was ordering large tequilas, no mixers.

The train home was less crowded than usual, probably because I'd stayed later and drunk more than usual, and had caught a later train. Perhaps I should do that more often?

Stephen would ask me how my day had been.

By the time I got home, however, he'd already eaten, and was up in his bedroom, typing. He had left my dinner in a low oven. There'd been times when I'd done that, when I – not

Stephen, who would have been a toddler – had cooked and kept food warm for Mary, while she worked late at the Faculty.

There would come a time, soon, when Stephen would not be there to do it.

I listened to the familiar clatter of Stephen's typewriter. I called hello, but did not go upstairs, did not disturb my son, who called back indistinctly that there was food, but did not come down to greet me.

How well we knew each other!

I used to dread the sound of Stephen typing. It weighed on me like the heavy stones Inquisitors used to place on the chests of suspected heretics: each time they breathed out, the weight compressed their lungs a little more, making it that much harder to breathe in. Whatever Stephen wrote I would have to read. Whatever he confessed, I would be obliged to know. Reading about Stephen's life was infinitely easier than discussing it, but that didn't entirely relieve my sense of doom.

Lately, however, the journal had become less and less about the minutiae of Stephen's life, and more and more about his grandfather. And, given our failure to find my father's diary and my lack of knowledge to pass on, it was mostly fiction. Which might have made it worse. I never read novels. Mary told me Plato banned poets from his republic, and I was with him there. If there'd been novelists around at the time, they'd have been out on their ears, too. Not because they lie, but because they play God. They make things happen for a purpose, dragging us towards an end that makes sense of everything that's gone before. In my work, it's only the perpetrators who believe in progress – or design. That's what Biology taught me: the survival of the fittest is not a story. It's a perpetual state of terror.

I was interested in Stephen's story, though. Not because I wanted to know the end – that much was given – but how was he going to get there? Would he try to offer an explanation? To plant the gun in the first act that would go off in the third? So far it didn't look like it. If I'd been Stephen's Eyquem, I might have murdered Jacobs, but I'm not sure I'd have killed myself.

At the Faculty we know most guns never go off at all. If they did, we'd all be dead.

That night, then, at the end of what had been, without question, a very bad day, the thrum of Stephen's typewriter felt almost comforting as I finished my lukewarm food and watched the late news on TV. The ceasefire had been renegotiated, but a bomb exploded in another marketplace on a different continent. A new film had opened; fans had queued all night to be amongst the first to see it, at least in this time zone. In local news, the police had stormed a flat in the east of the city. The reporter said the raid was intended to disrupt the operations of a major drugs network, and the police had taken away several crates of suspect material. One witness to the raid, a neighbour from the flat above, said they were a nice family and didn't seem to be the type. It just went to show, she said. Another said the police all had guns and bulletproof vests; some of them had no identification numbers on their uniforms. She'd noticed that.

The lottery jackpot had still not been won. Tomorrow's weather, as we headed towards Christmas, would be clear but cold.

I stiffened, a tiny shudder like a cold breeze passing across my skin. There had been no mention of the junior defence minister or his wife, which was only to be expected. But in the story of the supposed drugs arrests, the neighbour of the raided flat had said "family". That might have been slip of the tongue, but it didn't seem likely. The surveillance report had made no mention of a family.

I remembered Butler lifting her face from the pub table after several drinks. I was almost certain I'd seen tears in her eyes.

I had called her Brigid.

The day had been worse than I'd supposed.

# THE BASTARD

S HE *HAS* READ Woolf!
      She's read *To the Lighthouse* and *Mrs Dalloway* and
even says she's read *The Waves*. She's read *Orlando*, which I
hadn't even heard of. (I got away with it, though: I said: "As
in *Orlando Furioso*?" Which I haven't read, either, but neither
had she.)

But Woolf isn't the point. The point is how I know she's
read Woolf, which was just luck. We were queuing up for
lunch. I was with Barnett, who's like a puppy sometimes: an
annoying puppy who follows you around and thinks there's
nothing you want more than to play with him. She was behind
us in the queue with a friend. She spotted *Lighthouse* in my
jacket pocket and asked me what I thought of it. Out of
nowhere. I couldn't stop Barnett sniggering, but I ignored
him. Her friend – a girl I don't know with eye shadow and
long straight hair she must brush a thousand times a day –
wouldn't talk to Barnett. But we all took our plates and plastic
glasses and sat at the same table – on opposite sides, but, still,
the same table – and talked about Woolf. Barnett sniggered
some more and asked how many lesbians it takes to change
a light bulb; the girl with the long straight hair sneered; but,
still.

Her eyes are the pale green of fiddlehead ferns as they
unfurl.

"Do I have to go?"

"It's your turn, if you want to."

Eyquem had been down to the village last time, and possibly the time before that. The bed is in the corner, where Jacobs now lies, half dressed, half undressed, naked from the diaphragm to the knees, from where the long, grey-beige puttees he wears for extra winter insulation spiral down towards his feet. The puttees were bandages, and had once been white. Eyquem has told Jacobs that if he ever injures himself, he's going to have to use them, filthy as they are, because Eyquem is keeping the only sterile bandage they have left in the first aid box, along with the bottle of iodine and the large box of aspirin. But the pity of it is that Jacobs, despite his stupidity, his drunkenness whenever there is drink, and his ability to fall off the bicycle even when sober, despite the cack-handed way he handles the axe and the chisel, or fiddles with his hunting knife, throwing it at the wall or whittling sticks to nothing, despite all that Jacobs somehow never does manage to injure himself. He is like a cat, a child, a drunk: too supple, too unafraid to break his bones. On the first day of spring each year, when the stream to the south of the hut is no more than the first trickle of the coming thaw, Jacobs sits in the snow and dangles his legs in the icy water. He unwinds the soaking puttees and hangs them from the top of the beacon ladder, where they dry stiff and crisp and do not flutter in the strongest wind. His exposed calves are pale and flaccid things, almost indistinguishable from the dirty snow around the hut. Fleas and lice, stunned by the cold and sudden brilliant light, scatter from his skin like dandruff. "Life begins again!" he says, closing his eyes and leering at the sun.

"More's the pity," Eyquem says.

For now, it is still winter, and Jacobs' puttees remain tightly wound. But Christmas is not far away, little more than a week. They need supplies, Eyquem knows. They need oats and molasses and flour and pasta and coffee and tinned sardines and at least something special for Christmas, just as much as they need rehearsal time.

It is not his turn.

"Do you want to go?"

Jacobs idly scratches in his pubic hair. He takes his prick in his hand and for a moment Eyquem is afraid he will start to masturbate right then and there, while he is still in the room, trying to talk. But Jacobs lays it aside gently, precisely, like a patissier arranging delicate stock, and scratches the skin behind his scrotum instead.

"Or do you want me to?"

The alarm rings on the table in the centre of the room. Eyquem switches it off. He walks two steps to the south window, then proceeds clockwise around the hut: west, north, past Jacobs in the northeast corner, east.

The trouble is that Jacobs can never decide whether he thinks it's better to go down to the village, or stay up in the hut. It's a change, he says, two days away, of course. You have to give it that. Plus the chance of a drink and even a woman, if the Faculty hasn't cocked up the money order for their wages. But then you have to push it all back up the mountain, and that can be a bastard, especially in winter when it's mostly ice and snow up to the handlebars. Then again, he says, if you stay, you have to work forty-eight hours straight, the alarm going every thirty minutes, looking at fuck-all ninety-six times in a row without ever getting to sleep more than a nap. So no, he doesn't know.

"I'll go," Eyquem says. "You can learn your lines."

It is cold outside. The wind from the east slides between the buttons of his coat, through the gaps where the sleeves do not quite meet his gloves, but there has been little snow so far this year and, after a couple of hundred yards where the path is too steep to ride anyway, Eyquem mounts the bicycle and begins his perilous, skidding, arse-bouncing, knuckle-aching, vertebra-snapping descent. Every few minutes, he has to run into a tree or a rock, dismount, and catch his breath. It is an old bike, like Eyquem more at home on the boulevards of the metropolis, and not designed for such terrain. The brakes are not up to much. Sometimes it is easier just to fall off, especially in winter when snowdrifts usually soften the blow. But this year the path is icy and the snow's not thick enough to cushion a falling puppy. He has bruises he'll spend the rest of winter watching turn from blue to black to yellow. It will be entertainment of a kind.

It's good not to be in the hut, though. Good to see the mountains from a different angle. After an hour he is already too far down to see the beacons. He is out of the line of sight and cannot be held accountable. He can relax. As far as it is possible to relax when any moment he could be flung arse over tit from this old bicycle, with its solid rubber tyres and its ancient leather saddle that slices his gonads in two, when he could be catapulted clear over the handlebars, snap his spine and die, slowly, alone, the bicycle wheels spinning listlessly in the icy air. There is always some such price to be paid for a modicum of freedom, he thinks.

After another hour he takes a detour from the path into a stand of pines, where he falls onto the carpet of needles he is reasonably sure has lain undisturbed since he fell here this time last year. Or hereabouts, one pine tree looking so much like another. He picks himself up – nothing is broken, which is a blessing – picks up the bicycle and leans it against a trunk. It is late morning, but almost dark amongst the dense, chemical-scented trees. What little light penetrates to the forest floor is thick, like verdigris, like observing the world through the bottom of a wine bottle. There are trolls, as like as not, in woods like these: goblins. Or would be if he, like Jacobs, believed such nonsense.

Today, Eyquem thinks, he will not meet interference, ingratitude, insolence, disloyalty, ill-will or selfishness. Because today – and for all of tomorrow, at least until he returns, very late, laden with Christmas fare – he will be away from the hut, away from Jacobs.

He stretches into the deep pocket of his long overcoat, a relic of his student days that has served him well in his time as a watchman, mostly as an additional blanket whenever it is his turn to sleep. But when riding the bicycle it drags along the ground and snags in the wheels, and is not, to be honest, all that practical. From the pocket he pulls out a bag of raisins, the paper soft and creased. The bag is almost empty, the last of the raisins from the trip before the trip before last (the store does not always run to dried fruit). He has been holding them back, hiding them from Jacobs, anticipating just this moment, when he is on his way but not yet there, the steepest section completed, the path ahead about to level out until it runs, almost a road, if you can believe such a thing, into the village, a moment – this moment – when he can sit in the near-dark, out of sight, out of the wind, alone, close his eyes, tip back his head and feel the raisins' wrinkled skins soften on his tongue, the sweetness as he presses them against his teeth . . .

Bastard!

Eyquem spits out a potpourri of acorn cups and gravel.

"The bastard," he says aloud, "I'll kill him."

I'll poison his cereal. I'll slit his throat in his sleep. I'll chop off his head, scrape out his skull and use it for a shaving bowl. I'll shove a sharpened stick from his arse to his severed neck and roast him on a spit.

He won't. He knows he won't.

He's been in that hut too long.

He's been in that hut with Jacobs far too long.

Jacobs will be lying there now: scratching, farting, masturbating, ignoring the alarm – most likely not even setting the alarm – not watching for a signal. Who cares about signals, he'll be thinking, who gives a fig? Well, he would, Jacobs would, if ever there were a signal. If the fire on Cable's mountain, say, was lit and he didn't see it.

There won't be any signal.

Even now Cable will be readying himself – not to torch his beacon, but for the long, unfamiliar journey across shelterless tracts of moorland and barren mountainside. He'll be packing: food, a change of clothes, gifts, perhaps a bottle of brandy saved up all year? He would not be lighting his beacon and neither would his partner.

Eyquem doesn't know Cable, has no idea what kind of guest he'll make, much less what sort of actor he might prove to be. Still, it isn't much of a part. And he can have the script with him, in the bin.

Thinking about the play calms Eyquem with the promise of tasks to be completed: at the same time, it agitates him further. So much still depends on Jacobs, doesn't it? Looking out of the window, for instance. Jacobs can do that, of course

84

he can. But will he do it *right*? There are only two windows in the script, not four. And the timing? Would the timing be right? It seems unlikely. Eyquem hasn't timed a performance – they have barely rehearsed – but he is sure the 'looking out the window' moments in the play won't happen exactly on the half hour. That would be too much to hope for. Should he adapt the script? He can't do that. Could they adapt the timing of their observations to suit the script? That would be irregular. But surely it would be allowable, this once? Surely the Faculty could not object? At Christmas? But even then, it would still be down to Jacobs, wouldn't it? To get it right. Down to the bastard. And Eyquem is willing to bet he isn't learning his lines. He'll be lying in bed, right now, in the middle of the day, not reading the script, oh no, thumbing through his magazines, looking at women, or knives, or women with knives, his cock hard and upright, as upright as it ever gets.

Enough!

The bastard's doing it again.

No one should be surprised when a fig tree brings forth figs; or an arse, shit.

He will go on. The motion of the bicycle, now that the path is less precipitous, might calm him. It might. It is always possible.

It doesn't, though.

THE MORNING AFTER the bad day, Butler phoned in sick for the first time anyone could remember. Leach took the call. When he hung up, Simmons asked him how she was.

"Still drunk, I guess."

"But how was she?"

"I told her she didn't have to tell me," Leach said. "I'm not her boss. So she says, tell Gibbon for me. And I say, Gibbon's not here."

"But how was she?"

"How would I know?"

She returned to work the following day. She looked pale, still. But then, I thought, she'd always been pale. She had freckles.

She said she was going to resign.

"You can't resign."

"Three children. The nanny. A government minister and his wife."

"They're dead," said Leach.

"You're not helping," Simmons said, putting her arm around Butler's shoulders.

"I'm just saying. Resigning won't help."

Butler shrugged off Simmons' arm. "They killed each other. They slit each others' throats."

"They had no choice."

"How can I *not* resign?"

"You can't resign," I said.

It was true. It wasn't that I didn't want her to. It was just: this wasn't a job you resigned from. Surely she must know that, too?

"You can't resign," I said, again.

She sat at her desk, opened a file and turned the pages.

WOULD MY GRANDFATHER have used a word like "patissier"? Would he have known what a patissier was?

Of course. Just because he spent his life on a mountain doesn't make him a peasant. He wasn't born there. He lived in the city long enough to marry and have Dad. He probably read whatever he could – although I bet he never read *Orlando*, or women authors at all, except maybe George Eliot, who doesn't count. My grandfather would not have been a feminist. But he was a philosopher. I know it. Why else would he abandon his wife and child to stare at mountains and live with a man like Jacobs?

Sometimes I forget that I have invented Jacobs.

The bar has no name. It is the only place to buy a drink within two days' walk, so it has never needed one. The beer is foul, and the food worse, but at least it is beer, and food. There is the warmth of a fire, and windows that do not look out onto mountains. The vinegary smell of alcohol and burned peat rather than Jacobs' sweet smell of almonds and rotting toes.

"Evening."

"Afternoon."

The barman has begun to pour him a beer without asking. It isn't as if there's any choice.

"He hasn't slit your throat yet, then?"

"Who?"

The barman – a gormless, bald-headed excuse for a man with a beard like the dusty cobwebs of a giant, long-dead spider – chuckles incongruously. He places Eyquem's glass on the bar with the precision of a sculptor applying the final touches to a monumental statue of the gods.

He imitates Eyquem – "Who?" – and chuckles again.

Eyquem sips his beer and turns from the bar to find a table. It is the middle of the afternoon: too late, one might think, for lunch, too early to reward oneself after a long day's work. But there isn't much work round here, and the place is full. Each of a dozen small tables comes with a villager dribbling into his beer; most have two or three. It is December, after all. Outside, the snow is shovelled against the walls; ice double-glazes the windows and pushes the lids off water butts. It is getting dark at three o'clock. What else are they going to do?

"Twice in six weeks. We are blessed."

Mrs Slater. Rachel. He hadn't spotted her at the table by the fire, wiping Joseph's chin. Joseph, amongst a strong field, is the official village idiot. We all have our cross to bear, Mrs Slater says. She is the vicar's wife, so Eyquem supposes she must know what she's talking about.

He says, "It's almost Christmas."

"You don't say?"

She doesn't look too happy about it. Must be a busy time of year in her line of work, Eyquem thinks. Her husband's line, anyway. Eyquem never quite knows how to refer to the Reverend Slater. It seems wrong to call him Peter, even though it's his name. "Father" keeps suggesting itself, but he worries that only applies to priests. Papists. Is a vicar a priest? The

Pope is the Vicar of Rome, isn't he? Eyquem isn't sure, and it's never the right moment to ask.

"How's the . . . your husband. Must be busy?"

"Busy?"

"With Christmas and . . . everything."

"He has fuck-all to do at Christmas, leastways till midnight mass."

It would be fair to say that Mrs Slater – Rachel – is not what Eyquem had expected in a vicar's wife. Not that he'd ever met a vicar's wife before, but even so. The first time, he'd only been at the beacon for a couple of months; his son, Robert, was still wrapped tight and warm in his mother's womb, the pair of them blanketed against the city night, awaiting his letter home. Mrs Slater ("Please, call me Rachel") had offered to buy him a drink, and then another. He declined the second: he had not yet been paid and was unsure how far the Faculty's credit would run. She insisted. She told an old man with a hole in his face where his nose should have been to give up his place by the fire so that Eyquem could get properly warm. She touched his hand when she passed his drink across the table. She threw her head back when she laughed and the pink flesh of her throat startled him. She invited him to stay at the vicarage. It was their Christian duty, she told her husband later that evening, to save innocent visitors from the squalor of the room to rent above the bar – not to mention its lustful temptations, she said, with what Eyquem thought could surely not have been a wink in his direction? By then he had already accepted her offer, and it was obvious that her husband – as grey and cadaverous as his wife was florid and sensual – was not about to overrule her generosity. He smelled of sin forcibly repressed, she of face powder and fresh perspiration. He had already eaten, the Reverend Slater said.

There was some bread left, a little cheese, if they were hungry. She said, "We'll manage." He wished them both good night. She fried sausages and eggs and cakes of potato and cabbage seasoned with caraway. Eyquem had tasted nothing like it since he left the city. In fact, he'd tasted nothing much at all. Jacobs lived on oats and molasses. She reached across the table to wipe grease from his lips, then licked it from her fingers.

Later, she brought a clean towel to his room, and sat beside him on the bed. It creaked like a rusty hinge.

"Mrs Slater . . ."

"Rachel."

"Rachel. Mrs Slater. I am a married man."

"And I'm a married woman. We were made for each other."

"But I really am," Eyquem said. "Married. I'm going to be a father. My wife is going to have a baby."

"And yet, here you are."

Is that how it would have happened? Is that what Granddad would have said?

Or would he have said nothing, hoping she wouldn't notice the pale band of flesh around his finger where he had slipped off his wedding ring earlier that evening? Or hoping that she would, and see it as an invitation?

I don't know.

Dad never talks about why Granddad left the city. How would he know?

The Faculty sent him there, to the beacon.

But surely there was some choice? His or theirs. Some exception to be made for a man about to start a family?

I don't know.

I'm seventeen. How am I supposed to know?

# WHAT DO YOU SUPPOSE THEY
# THOUGHT ABOUT?

A WEEK LATER, the night there were no trains –
because we'd closed down all the stations – we were
drinking in the Butcher's anyway when Leach looked up from
his beer and said: "What do you suppose Butler does when
she's not here?"

I peered into my glass. It was empty. "Goes home to her
boyfriend."

"She has a boyfriend?"

He sounded alarmed, as if the thought had never occurred
to him before.

"I've no idea. Ask her."

"Right."

Leach drained his glass, looked over to the bar where
Simmons was getting the next round in.

"Do you suppose she has sex, though? Butler?"

"In general, or specifically instead of coming to the pub?"

He thought about it.

"Specifically. Do you suppose she's having sex now? With
her boyfriend, whoever he is. Right now?"

"At six-thirty on a Wednesday evening?"

"Yes."

"No."

"No?"

"I doubt it."

He looked relieved, but what did I know? It had been fifteen years since I'd had sex at any time of day. I couldn't say I'd missed it.

I did know I would much prefer Leach not to talk about her. Or about anyone, really. But especially not her. Butler. Brigid.

Butler was wherever she was when she wasn't with the rest of us in the pub. Except that now, since the junior defence minister, and the junior defence minister's wife and family, she was drinking again. We'd all seen her. Simmons said she threw up in the ladies' toilets and then again in the taxi home. So why wasn't she in the Butchers with the rest of us?

Simmons squeezed her way back from the bar carrying three pints. The pub was more crowded than usual, despite the lack of trains. Or because of the lack of trains. It felt like the end of term. Bring your own toys in. Or perhaps the end of the world.

Simmons placed the drinks on the table. None of us said Cheers.

Leach said, "What do you suppose they thought about?"

"Who?"

"The children. When the mother . . ." he interrupted himself, "you know . . ." he pointed to his throat "the daughter? What do you suppose went through their minds?"

Simmons turned to me. "If I smash this glass and kill him with it, will you be a character witness?"

"And when the father . . ." Leach pointed to his throat again, "the mother. What was he thinking? What was the father thinking?"

Simmons and I said nothing.

Leach took a swig at his new pint. "They say your whole

93

life flashes in front of your eyes before you die."

"Not flashes," I said. "Crawls."

"I'm sure they say flashes."

"They're wrong."

"How do you know?"

"Because it's all before you die. That's what life is: a series of tableaux. Snippets. Occasional action scenes. Before you die."

Leach raised his glass. "Cheers," he said, then.

It was our fourth pint. Normally we left after two. Three would be easier. With three it would always be obvious whose turn it was, who hadn't put his hand in his pocket. Having two, we always had to carry one over to the next day or somebody – it would be Leach, obviously – would wind up never buying a round, or trying not to, and Simmons or I would have to bring it up. But that night we'd had three and then Simmons offered to buy another.

The thing was, there weren't any trains, so . . . we could all have left at any time, because there was no particular time we had to leave, as there usually was, to catch our trains. But then again, there was no particular time we had to leave to catch our trains, because there were no trains, so . . . we hadn't left. And now we'd have to remember who hadn't bought a second round. Unless we made it to six pints, of course. Or nine.

Nine!

When had I last drunk nine pints?

I must have done, once. When I was a student. About the time my father died.

The thing was, even though there was no particular time we had to leave, when we did leave, there would be no trains and we would have to walk. To be able to walk. Five miles, in my case. More, I thought, for Leach and Simmons, though I wasn't exactly sure where either of them lived. So drinking nine pints was definitely out of the question. Or even six, at my age. This would have to be the last, in fact.

There were no trains because someone had rung in credible bomb threats for five of the city's railway terminals, and we'd closed them down. We'd closed the sixth and seventh, too, for good measure, in case it was a trick. In case that was where the real bombs were, which was how she'd do it, Simmons said, if she were doing it. And we'd had to admit she had a point.

Butler had left the way she always did, on her bicycle.

By then, we knew the threats weren't real, but it was already too late: the stations were all closed and it would be midnight before the mess got straightened out. They wouldn't put on special services then because that would just screw up the schedules for the morning and prolong the chaos. So the decision was – not even a decision, now, just standard operating procedure – to write the whole thing off and let everyone sort themselves out, again.

"It's your round," Leach said.

"I can't."

"Of course you can."

Simmons said, "I rang home before we left the office. MydaughterNicola's looking after her dad. Your Stephen will be all right, won't he?"

I hadn't even thought about Stephen.

In the corner of the pub the TV played silent news.

I said, "Do you ever buy lottery tickets?"

The lottery had been in the news for the past few weeks. On my usual walk home, on the road up from the station to my house, there was a cherry tree that grew out of the pavement at forty-five degrees. It must have been leant on as a

95

sapling. Each time I passed, I had to duck. At which point, for no reason I could ever fathom, I would wonder what I would do if I won the lottery. It was a meaningless tic, an involuntary association. I never bought tickets then, never watched the draw. But there had been a time, fifteen years earlier, when I'd bought one every week, and checked religiously to see if it had won. I picked the same numbers every time, numbers based on dates I could not forget, even now: my father's death; Stephen's birth; Mary's death; her due date.

The jackpot had not been claimed for almost two months and stood at sixty million, give or take. Walking home from the pub – not the station – I would not pass the tree, would not think of the lottery. Except that now I had. The news had made me think about the tree, anticipate the moment when I ducked under it and thought about winning the lottery, a moment that would not now happen.

What would I have done if I'd won sixty million? Or six?

What did anybody do? They said it wouldn't change them. They said they'd go back to work as usual, then left their jobs, bought new houses and new cars. They gave money to charity, took lovers, or bought prostitutes; they got divorced, gambled, drank and drugged themselves into an early grave. Or not. Most of them were fine. That is, they died just like everybody else.

What if I had won, back then? When for a few months I'd bought a ticket at the end of every week?

It had already been too late, even then.

I might have killed myself. I might have drunk myself to death. It was possible. It was always possible, of course. But fifteen years later, I knew there was no rush. It would always be too late.

Isn't that what Mary always said?

"Exley?"

Leach's voice reached me through the background throb of chattering, drunken, train-less commuters.

"Exley?"

"What?"

"It's still your round."

I capitulated. Five pints, five miles. There was a certain fitness to it.

DAD HASN'T MADE it home tonight. On the news they said there were no trains. He hasn't rung, but there might have been no signal, either. Sometimes they close it down. There was nothing on the news but there must have been a bomb, or several bombs – or, more likely, threats of bombs – so he'll be busy, and then he'll have to walk. I've told him he should get a bike. One of those fold-up jobs he could carry up to the office. Then, when everything shuts down, he'd be all right. He could come home.

The noise was worse than ever this afternoon. About three, four o'clock. It just went on and on. When it started – not today: when it first started – I thought next door were hanging a picture, putting up shelves. Then I thought maybe it was some sort of exercise routine, that they'd got one of those machines, and it was knocking against the wall. But surely, that would have had some rhythm? As it is, it's just too random. If there were a code it would have to repeat, wouldn't it? There would be patterns. I've asked Dad, but it never seems to happen when he's here.

In Greek today we started the *Oresteia*. Mr Hawkins says we should put it on at the end of term, to help us really understand the plays. She'll be Clytemnaestra, I know. Or Electra. One of them.

Will I be Orestes?

We'll see.

"A cold coming you had of it," Eyquem says when Brooks stands in the doorway, stamping the compacted snow from his boots and allowing the icy air to rush flakes into the hut and scatter them like crowds when the first shot is fired.

"A cold coming . . . yes. Very good."

Eyquem isn't sure if Brooks has recognized the allusion or is just being polite.

It is Christmas Eve. Brooks has come from the north, with the wind at his back. He is a large, florid man who greets Eyquem as "the little dog" and tells Jacobs he's never forgotten the time he and Eyquem and that other chap – what was his name? – all lost at Monopoly to the man from his north who, funnily enough, was called North.

"I was the top hat."

Jacobs says nothing.

Brooks unrolls his bedding neatly and lays his clean clothes in a small pile at one end as a pillow. He asks if there is anything he can do to help. He does not look surprised when Eyquem hands him a copy of the script and tells him which part he is to play. He flips through the slim book with interest.

"In a bin?" he asks, cheerfully enough.

He has brought biscuits.

Jacobs is all for opening the tin immediately; Eyquem says they should leave it for the feast; for Christmas Day. It's a big tin, Brooks points out; there will be plenty to go around. So the three of them nibble a biscuit each and watch Cable slowly inch his way towards them from the west and up the snow-bound mountain.

"What's he lugging up here?"

Whatever it is looks heavy, and makes the already arduous task of manoeuvring his bicycle up the icy path more challenging still. The blustery wind, too, keeps shoving him southwards, away from the path. As he comes closer, they can see the effort with which he keeps the bike upright, no matter how much it skids and slips on the treacherous terrain. Closer still, they can make out, strapped to either side of the rear wheel like outsized panniers, two enormous glass bottles, or jars, or flagons: straight-sided, stiff-shouldered, with tiny round finger holds, like ears, on either side of their short, stubby necks.

Eyquem racks his brains. There is a word, he knows. A word for those bottles, although he has no context, no idea how he knows it.

Cable leans his bike against the wall of the hut and bursts the door wide open.

"Ta-da!" he shouts.

He holds forth one of the enormous glass jars, presenting it to them, or them to it, Eyquem isn't sure.

*Demijohn*, he thinks.

"I bring you . . . whisky!" Cable announces.

Jacobs eyes the bottle dubiously. "It's clear," he says.

"As the crystal streams of Heaven."

Cable strides into the hut and places his treasure carefully in the centre of the table.

If this a demijohn, Eyquem thinks, is there such a thing as a whole john? A Jonathan, perhaps?

"When you distill whisky," Cable continues, "it's always clear – it's been distilled! Now, do you know why it goes that orange-browny colour?"

Eyquem isn't going to ask, doesn't want to encourage the man, but can't stop Jacobs.

"Why?"

"Because they put it in dirty barrels."

Cable pauses for an expression of disbelief or – better yet – disgust, but gets none. They are a harder crowd than that to please, even Jacobs.

"Sherry barrels."

Another pause. Eyquem thinks the man has missed his calling. He should have been a mountebank.

"They put it in dirty sherry barrels and they leave it there getting dirtier and dirtier, leaching all that sherry-filth into the precious whisky. The dirtier it is, the more they expect us to pay." He shakes his head, then goes back outside to fetch the second bottle, letting in more snow as he goes, and as he returns.

"An alien people clutching their gods," Brooks says, and Eyquem is impressed.

"It's a racket," Cable continues, as if there had been no interruption. "If I wanted to drink sherry, I'd buy sherry. But who the fuck wants sherry?"

There is no question of leaving the whisky for Christmas Day.

"Why d'you think I brought two?"

There are no glasses, but they each have a tin mug. Cable pours, carefully lifting and tilting the heavy demijohn, making the others hold their mugs at an angle, to stop the whisky splashing out too fast, then straightening them up to catch the final drops. They wait until he has finished, out of nerves, perhaps, or a sense of occasion.

"To the beacons!" Cable raises his own mug carefully. "May they stay unlit forever!"

"The beacons," murmur Brooks and Jacobs.

Eyquem and Brooks sip cautiously; Cable and Jacobs swig.

Jacobs chokes and coughs, his face turns red, his feet stamp at the floor. "Wrong way!" he sputters through his fist.

It tastes, Eyquem thinks, surprisingly like whisky.

"I'm no connoisseur," Brooks says, smiling at each of them in turn, smiling at the whole hut, at the view to the surrounding mountains, "but this really isn't bad."

"I'm no conny-sewer, neever," Jacobs hams, recovering from his choking fit and holding out his mug for more. "But I know it's gunna get me pissed."

"Well, this is cosy," Cable says, dropping into the chesterfield and sinking down until he is almost horizontal, whisky mug balanced on his chest. "What are you all eating?"

"I brought biscuits. Would you like one?"

Brooks holds out the tin. Cable pulls out a fistful. Crumbs scatter across his clothes.

"No chocolate?"

Eyquem takes the tin from Brooks, replaces the lid, and puts it on a high shelf above the sink.

At that moment, the alarm rings.

"Christ on a hairy bicycle!" Cable jerks up, scattering crumbs and spilling whisky on the worn cushions of the chesterfield.

Eyquem switches off the alarm. He steps to the south window. It is almost dark outside, but the snow on the mountainside still glows with the last of the light. He walks to the west window, then to the north – where he stands in front of the chesterfield to see out. Cable says, "You're still doing that?" Eyquem says nothing, but walks to the east window, then back to the centre of the hut, where he resets the alarm clock.

"It's Christmas," Cable says. "A holiday."

"We're still on duty. Me today; Jacobs tomorrow."

Jacobs peers into his mug, but says nothing.

Cable says, "But nothing's going to happen."

"We can't know that."

"It's Christmas. Nothing happens. Okay, mankind is saved, but nothing actually happens. No one stirs. Not even a mouse. If anyone lights a beacon it'll be because they're pissed."

"That's a point," Brooks says. "It's unlikely anything will happen now."

"We watch for signals," Eyquem says. "If there's a signal we pass it on. Christmas makes no difference."

"That's true, too," says Brooks. "*I watch for the signal-fire, the light breaking out of Troy, shouting Troy is taken. So she commands, full of her high hopes.*"

"What?" says Jacobs.

"*That woman,*" Eyquem says, "*she manoeuvres like a man.*"

"Who?" says Cable. "What woman?"

"Clytemnaestra," Brooks says. "The wife of Agamemnon."

"What the fuck?"

"Aeschylus. *The Oresteia.*"

"And?"

"She's waiting for Agamemnon to get home from the siege of Troy."

"But what if it's not a signal?" Cable sits up again, warming to his theme, trying to get the conversation back to his own territory. "What if it's just some poor sod who's had one too many, trips over his bootlaces, smashes a paraffin lamp and burns down his hut? I left Burton to come here, and Burton's a moron. He could burn the hut down even when he's sober. So what do we do, in a couple of hours, say, when we've had some more of this" – he waves his mug towards the whisky on the table – "what happens if we see a fire on my mountain, eh?"

"We light the beacon. We pass on the signal."

"But it wouldn't be a signal."

"We wouldn't know that."

"I'd know."

"You wouldn't *know*. At best you might guess."

"And if I'm right? And we pass on a signal that isn't a signal?"

"It's not our job to guess."

As their voices become more emphatic, Brooks looks increasingly uncomfortable. "It's your beacon, Eyquem. We're your guests. I suggest we leave it to you."

Eyquem says nothing.

"Well, Jacobs," says Cable after a moment's silence. "What do you say?"

Jacobs winds himself up to speak. It seems the wheels have been turning slowly in his brain. "What happens when the woman sees the signal? When Aga-whatsit's on his way?"

Brooks says, "She welcomes him home."

"And then?"

"She murders him," Eyquem says.

"Nice," says Cable.

"He killed their daughter," Brooks says. "Sacrificed her to the gods."

Eyquem says, "So Orestes, the girl's brother, kills his mother to avenge his father."

"And they all live happily ever after," Cable says. "What's for dinner?"

Three hours later, they have eaten the tinned sardines Eyquem hauled up from the village, together with the cod roes that belonged, by rights, to the Reverend Slater, but which Rachel had slipped into his greatcoat pocket on the morning of his departure (whilst straightening his scarf and wishing him safe journey, happy Christmas, and squeezing his penis surreptitiously through his clothes); they have drunk perhaps a shade over half of the first demijohn of whisky when the alarm rings for the sixth time since Cable's arrival. After the first, he had merely sighed, more loudly than was strictly necessary, as Eyquem stood, each thirty minutes, and walked clockwise around the hut – inside at first and then, once darkness fell and the windows showed nothing but lamp-lit reflections, outside – pausing at each cardinal point and seeing nothing. But Cable is used to his own whisky, and is not as drunk as he appears. On this, the sixth instance, he is waiting. As the hammer hits the bell his hand shoots out and grabs the clock from the table. He jumps to his feet and holds it high above his head, stretching up on tiptoes, like a child tormenting a younger sibling.

"Come and get it!"

Eyquem, who is taller than Cable and could, no doubt, have reached the clock however high Cable stretched, nonetheless ignores him. He goes outside, closing the door carefully behind him. Cable throws the clock at the stove. The glass shatters. The alarm bell rattles and falls silent. He picks up his whisky and refills all their mugs, including Eyquem's. When Eyquem returns, Cable says, "So. What are we doing tomorrow? To celebrate?"

Eyquem pulls out a wooden box from beneath the bed and digs out a fourth copy of the script. He hands it to Cable.

He takes out, too, a large hourglass, one bulbous end half full of turquoise sand. He sets it on the shelf next to the biscuit tin. The sand begins to trickle through in a thin, barely perceptible stream.

He points to Cable's script. "That's you."

If you watch, Eyquem knows, you can see the sand pile up at the bottom, while, at the top, nothing seems to change.

So THAT'S WHAT it felt like to drink nine pints?
Shit.

More precisely, that's what it felt like to *have drunk* nine
pints and then slept, insofar as I slept at all, on the office
floor. At the time, drinking the eighth and ninth, I'd thought
it merely unpleasant, and stupid. I'd felt very full. But waking
up on the thin grey carpet tiles beneath my desk there was no
doubt whatever in my mind that what I felt was: shit.

I needed water.

I needed air.

I didn't need air. I needed the toilet.

When I levered myself upright and completed a long, slow
trek across the office, I found Leach asleep in one of the stalls,
his trousers around his ankles, his head slumped back over
the cistern.

I needed breakfast.

I looked at my watch. It was twenty to six. In the morning,
I assumed, although it was hard to tell. The windows of the
Faculty were covered with heavy netting, like suburban lace
curtains grown dense with age and soot. It was supposed to
keep us safe from bombs, as well as prying eyes. I don't know
how much difference it would have made to shrapnel, but
barely any light got through. We worked by fluorescent bulbs
at noon in high summer. And now it was December. At 5.40
it would be dark outside, am or pm.

It must have been morning, though. I couldn't have slept all day. My bladder would never have allowed it. Butler would have woken us. She would have brought coffee, or water and alka seltzer.

My stomach churned at the thought.

I couldn't get breakfast yet.

Leach would have a terrible stiff neck, I thought, slumped like that. But I couldn't face the thought of waking a hungover, half-naked Leach who would no doubt feel as bad as I did, or worse, and would still be Leach, to boot. I left him in peace and returned to the office.

Simmons was stretched out under her own desk, using the little foam orthopaedic cushion from her office chair as a pillow. Her mouth was open and she was snoring, but gently, a soft and comforting sound. I thought she looked vulnerable. It was not a word I could recall ever having associated with her before.

Baconandmushroomsandwich.

Baconandmushroom.

Bacon.

And mushroom. And egg and sausage and tea. Lots of tea. The café would not open for another hour.

I should drink water and get more sleep.

I looked at the stretch of stained and threadbare carpet beneath my desk. I would get no more sleep there.

It occurred to me that the offices were empty. Not entirely empty, of course. The duty desk would be manned; the China office would be humming, given the time difference; there would be pale, crepuscular stalwarts minding their machines in the frozen Crypt, where it was neither night nor day. Warren himself might be there. He must live somewhere,

I supposed – somewhere else – but I couldn't envisage him above ground, leaving the building, going home, *having* a home. This part of the building, though – this floor and the floors above – would all be empty.

Gibbon's office would be empty.

Gibbon's office had been empty for a while, of course, since he'd disappeared. But just then, at 5.45am – I was sure it was am – there would be no one at the assistants' desks, either, no one on that entire floor who might wonder what I was doing in my Divisional Director's office at a quarter to six in the morning, when there was no one there.

What would I be doing?

Snooping.

Investigating.

Showing an interest.

And there's the rub, I thought. I would not go upstairs, would not slip unobserved into Gibbon's office and rifle through his filing cabinets and desk drawers in search of clues to the cause of his disappearance, and the likelihood of his ever returning, because I didn't care. It would be foolish to squander my indifference – to take the step towards involvement, culpability and murder – on grounds so trivial.

Who cared what had happened to Gibbon?

Gibbon, presumably: although not if what had happened was that he was dead. Mrs Gibbon, possibly – his wife or mother, if either existed and was not already dead herself. (I had no idea.)

Simmons?

We all assumed, I think, that Simmons would be taking Gibbon's job. But why? Because she appeared a bit more capable, more organized, more responsible than the rest of us? Because she had asked me to take one of her cases, rather than simply allowing her backlog to slide, as Leach or I might have done? Because it might yet turn out to be a booby-trap designed to suck me in and bog me down and ultimately spit me out, having shredded what little professional credibility I might possess?

Where had the case come from in the first place?

Where had Butler's case come from? The junior minister and his oil executive wife?

I listened to Simmons snore, a faint sound like a nesting hamster. Perhaps she had just been busy?

What difference did it make?

The trouble with indifference was that it took such constant vigilance to maintain. I wasn't convinced I had the energy. I might as well go straight upstairs and rummage around in Gibbon's paperwork.

Which is what I did.

# WHAT MATTERS IS, IT HAPPENS

In the morning Eyquem wakes the other three
– Jacobs in the bed in the corner, Cable on the ancient
chesterfield, Brooks in his sleeping roll on the floor – with
mugs of fresh coffee. Porridge bubbles thickly in a large, black-
ened pot on the stove.

"Happy Christmas," Brooks says.

On the table in the middle of the room, the first demijohn
stands empty; the second remains almost full, like a threat.
Beside them, the last grains of sand trickle through the hourglass again.

Eyquem prods Jacobs' inert body through layers of blankets and overcoats. "It's your shift."

Jacobs groans, but does not move.

Cable groans. He sips his coffee. "It needs a drop of something in it. That'll put us straight."

Eyquem prods Jacobs again.

"All right, all right."

Jacobs pushes back the covers and swings his legs out of
bed. A foul miasma rises from his groin before dissipating in
the general odour of the hut. He groans again as his head rises
from the horizontal. He has rolled his trousers up to make
a pillow; he unrolls them now and pulls them, grunting and
straining, over his grey puttees and shapeless underpants. He
shuffles to the north window, leaning against the chesterfield
for support.

"Get that out of my face," Cable shouts.

If Jacobs hears him, he gives no sign, but shuffles to the west, lingering by the stove in the corner before moving reluctantly on to complete a perfunctory anti-clockwise circuit, barely opening his eyes. Outside, sunlight ricochets off the icy landscape with forensic brilliance. Jacobs drops into a wooden chair, reaches out and turns over the hourglass. He crosses his arms on the table and lays his head on them.

"Where are those dark glasses?"

"They're a prop," Eyquem says.

"I need a prop."

"Breakfast first, then we'll begin."

Brooks finishes rolling and re-tying his bedclothes. He pulls a small brocaded bag from the depths of his greatcoat pocket.

"Which way?"

"North, then south."

"I thank you."

He opens the door. Ice-cold air sweeps through the hut, bleaching the fetid atmosphere. Stepping over the threshold, Brooks pauses to stretch and yawn.

Cable growls. "Were you born in a fucking barn?"

After breakfast – Cable takes whisky in his porridge and his coffee; Jacobs does the same – the four men feel much better. When the hourglass empties, Jacobs actually looks out of the windows before confirming there is nothing to see. Cable suggests arm wrestling. Brooks has brought a set of dominoes, and a ukulele. Eyquem outlines his plan for the day.

When he has finished, Cable leaves a pause before saying, "In a bin?"

Eyquem nods.

"Why?"

"Because that's what the script says. You and Brooks."

Cable turns to Brooks. "And you're okay with this?"

"It might be fun."

Cable lifts an eyebrow, but says nothing.

"It's my choice," Eyquem says. "That's the way it works. We're hosting this year, and I choose this."

"And I choose this," says Cable, topping up his coffee mug with whisky.

"It's not hard. You can sit in the dark most of the time. You won't have much to do."

"But what's the point?"

"It's a play. A performance."

"Who's going to see it?"

"That's not the point."

Cable sets down his whisky and holds up his hands like a barrister drawing the court's attention to the evident idiocy of the argument they are being invited to accept.

"Not *the point?*"

It is a shame, Eyquem thinks. The man is a natural actor. Perhaps he should have a bigger part? But no, it would be too risky. He hasn't even read the script.

"It's a performance. A cry in the dark, if you will. It doesn't matter who sees." Before Cable can object that no one ever sees a cry - in the dark or otherwise - Eyquem corrects himself. "Or hears. If no one sees, or hears, at all. What matters is, it happens. That we prove we're human, and alive."

"By sitting in a bin?"

"If that's what the script calls for, yes."

At this point Jacobs interjects, pointing out to Cable that

while he and Brooks will be sitting in bins, Eyquem himself will be on the chesterfield.

Cable apes outrage. "No way. That's not right."

"And I'll be pushing him around on it."

"No fucking way."

"Oh come on, gents," says Brooks. "Let's give it a go."

Astonishingly, they do. Perhaps it is the implicit threat of the alternative – of Brooks' ukulele in particular – or perhaps Cable's griping resistance is no less a performance than the one Eyquem has in mind, a way of doing something, rather than nothing.

It is Christmas, after all.

Together they shuffle the table and the chesterfield, placing the latter at the exact centre of the hut. They fetch the two metal dustbins Eyquem has washed out – the last drops of water have subsequently frozen, but are easily enough chipped off – and place them, side-by-side, in the southeast corner. Brooks and Cable take their places, not without complaint on Cable's part, but nonetheless without undue resistance. Eyquem hands each of them his script, then puts the lids in place. Immediately there is a loud knocking from Cable's bin. Eyquem lifts the lid.

"It's dark in here."

"Of course."

"How am I supposed to see the script?"

Eyquem thinks briefly. "You only have lines when your lid is off."

"But I won't know what's going on."

The lid on Brooks' bin rises, balanced on his head like a galvanized sun hat. He says, "It's a fair point. How will we follow our cues?"

Jacobs says, "We could give you candles."

The bins quickly fill with smoke and Cable sets fire to his eyebrows.

"We could do without the lids."

"No," says Eyquem.

"We could pretend. Act."

"No. The script is very particular."

"We could cut holes to let the light in."

"It's Faculty property."

"The Faculty will never know."

"Rats might get in, afterwards, and nest."

"Rats? Up here?"

It is another reasonable point. Eyquem has to admit that Cable, although difficult, is not stupid. Nothing larger than a flea survives up there. Fleas and lice and men. And the fleas and lice only survive because of the men. Because of them.

They cut holes in the bin lids.

Brooks consults the first page of his script. "You can't put a sheet over the bins, or the holes will be no use."

"We haven't got a sheet," Jacobs points out.

"We'll have to pretend," Cable says.

Eyquem lets that go.

Brooks and Cable get back in the bins, Cable giving a double thumbs-up sign as he sinks slowly out of sight. Eyquem puts the lids back in place. He checks the hourglass. There is perhaps two minutes' worth of sand left. He checks the placement of the chesterfield again, and sits dead centre on its lumpy, under-stuffed and threadbare cushions. He puts on the dark glasses and pulls the stained handkerchief from his pocket. He leans back and drops the handkerchief over his face. He holds up his right hand, three fingers extended, then slowly folds each finger down: three, two, one.

The sand in the hourglass stops trickling through.

Nothing happens.

"Go," Eyquem whispers from under the handkerchief.

"Go where?" says Jacobs.

"*Start.*"

Jacobs consults his script. He shuffles over to the west window, peers out, and begins to shuffle back.

"You're supposed to laugh," Eyquem hisses.

"What's there to laugh at?"

"Just do it. Start again and do exactly what the script says."

Jacobs peers suspiciously at the script again. "It *says* I should have a stepladder."

"You don't need a ladder to see out of our windows."

"But . . ."

Eyquem lifts the handkerchief from his face and turns to look at Jacobs. "You don't need a ladder."

"But I do need to laugh?"

"Yes."

Jacobs thinks for a moment. "Why?"

"Because you can. We haven't got a ladder. We haven't got any sheets. But you *can* laugh. It doesn't take any special equipment."

He lays his head back and drops the handkerchief back over his face.

"Go," he says. "Action."

Jacobs shuffles back to the west window.

"Ha, ha," he says.

He shuffles across the hut to the east window and peers out.

"Ha-ha, ha."

He goes to the bins, lifts Brooks' lid and peers inside.

"Ha-ha, ha-ha."

From under the handkerchief Eyquem hisses, "*Brief* laugh. Brief."

Jacobs replaces Brooks' lid and lifts Cable's.

"Ha-ha."

"Ha-haaarrh, Jim lad," Cable replies.

Jacobs replaces the lid, walks back across the hut to the door, where he turns to face south, where the audience would be, if there were an audience.

"Finished, it's finished," he says, grandly.

"Good," says Cable, standing abruptly as his bin lid clatters to the floor. "Time for a drink."


It is raining. I can hear it on the window. It is late and I should really be in bed. There are no trains and Dad will be walking home. It is very cold and the rain is turning to sleet. He'll be all right. Rain always sounds worse from indoors.

WHEN I RETURNED from breakfast Simmons said, "You look terrible." Which surprised me because, after a great deal of fried food and several mugs of tea, I certainly felt much better. The itching in my legs had calmed down, for one thing. I couldn't remember having scratched since I'd left the building. Perhaps I was fooling myself, though. Simmons looked exactly as if she'd spent the night on the floor beneath her desk. As did Leach, which was unfair, in the circumstances. Only Butler, when she arrived, folding bike in one hand and her hair still damp from the shower, looked like someone ready to spend the day working – rather than, say, begging tramps to share their meths and provide directions to a decent flophouse. When the telephone on my desk rang, it was Butler who intercepted the call, while I stared uncomprehendingly at the vibrating instrument and wondered where that awful noise was coming from.

She pressed the receiver to her ear with one hand, holding a finger to her lips with the other. After a while she said, "He's a bit tied up right now. He'll call you back."

She hung up.

"That was Operations. He said you'd want to talk to him."

When I didn't reply, she said, "I'll make coffee."

Operations. It could only be about the raid, the one we'd told the press was looking for drugs. Simmons' case.

I unlocked my desk drawer, scraping it against the renewed

itching in my thighs, and pulled out the initial sit rep Ops had sent through on the afternoon of the raid. It seemed clear cut: unusually so. Traces of presumed explosives, yes. Chemical residues duly bagged and sent for analysis. But that was hardly the point. They'd found homemade C4: literally, bricks of the stuff. An entire false wall of plastic explosive, papered over with tourist posters of palaces and parliaments, ruins of the ancient world, behind which they'd found more explosives, the makeshift lab in which it had been manufactured, a collection of large and complicated knives, a couple of semi-automatic pistols, an assault rifle, and money. Lots of money. Two suitcases: not briefcases, not attaché cases, but two of those vast trolleys whole families can barely lift onto the conveyor belts at check-in, one bursting with cash, the other perhaps three-quarters full – although just how much there might have been before the journey to the evidence inventory was a matter of conjecture.

I also re-read the file note I'd written earlier. I could now discount Scenario 1: there was no way this could be a genuine, 24-carat crock of shit. Scenario 5 – the genuine but isolated threat – was also looking shaky. That much materiel – and that much money – was unlikely to be the property of a disaffected teenager with a taste for leather overcoats. Scenarios 2 to 4, variants on the theme of a fake plot were still viable – this *could* be a set-up – but only by someone with access to the goods who was willing to absorb the inevitable loss of a little overhead along the way. Someone in the Faculty, then; or in another organization with reciprocal lending rights. Which didn't exactly narrow it down. But who would go to all that trouble – risk all that hardware and cash – just to discredit Simmons (Scenario 2), or me (Scenario 3)?

I couldn't see that either of us was worth it.

Which left Scenario 4 – the major distraction from something truly frightening somewhere else – and Scenario 6, the genuine, organized threat to be investigated, tracked down and disrupted.

In other words: the worst of all possible worlds. One where I could not avoid doing something – which was bad enough – but where any action I might take could be cataclysmically, provably, wrong.

Gibbon – and Gibbon's predecessor – might have spouted the cliché about our side having to be right every time, but that didn't make it true. The only way we could keep being right was to be wrong over and over and over again. To stack the odds in our favour. And even then, we'd get it wrong.

Butler had got it wrong, hadn't she?

And while the Directors talked about eradicating the blame culture and treating our mistakes as learning opportunities, they didn't mean it.

I lifted the receiver on my phone, put it down again. I went to the toilet and splashed more water on my face. My arse was itching now. My *arse*.

Perhaps after lunch?

Perhaps right now I should pop down to the Crypt? I hadn't been home and had nothing new for Warren to decode, but yesterday's script would be waiting for me.

I wasn't sure I was up to the latest instalment. At some point – some point soon, no doubt – Stephen would get round to wondering why his grandfather left a young, pregnant wife to become a beacon keeper. Worse still, he'd wonder what I – the product of that pregnancy – felt about it. Would *that* be the gun in his first act? He would make suppositions. He would put words in my mouth, thoughts in my head, emotions. And I would have to read it.

Better, on the whole, to get on with the job.

I left the toilets, returned to my desk, and rang Operations. While I waited for an answer I wondered again about what I'd found in Gibbon's office, and what, if anything, it meant. Then I was through. A man I'd never met, but to whom I'd often spoken, was gabbling in my ear. Explaining. Excusing. There was a note of contrition in his voice, but also one of aggressive self-defence: after all, it *had* been an impressive haul. They had obviously intercepted a major threat.

When I could get a word in, I said: "What do you mean, the wrong flat?"

My *arse*, for pity's sake.

12231238765123 5014b518959187519517581251723051923751293512 3591
02375712983591235897190238501723580123790581289357917239578
912375121231234912737379123819283749734789237428374127394198
237481329047123471238401723471238947123491723941 82347192374
01723471273481234812903471283904198237490172937 4091273094
81209374091823984710293749871239479812374901729374917234
0812937490123894719023840918230947109238491293740 9172309
48190234971290347918239407190238409172309471927 3409
172934790127340917293047172349071029347192374901723 9471
923749817239471923740182340917230948102934102834 90123
04810238409183417239048019832401972340981820349128 34091
82390847190237408127349179028347109723491820347198 23409
17290340912347108923748912379410982374098172341897 230471
09237417234709123401023414902394123491029347128934 710239
4712340983290747981079234079179234981023947012384 012934
89172939123904123984239748123483240919348123423847 1234236
412395265814976168419234172581834017231732481341834 1238412
38412386182349162316237123612346127341327412341234 127348123
41234172384710923717293570173571832412846790237 4612937172
34791273491273491034
32498192034012341293840134193284123412
340182394891283904812384128347812634612347123496 1234123
41213894823481236486234608 6484

# ONE

"**W**HAT'S HE READING now?"
He'd been reading all his life. But when I tried
to picture him with a book in his hand this week, last week
– anytime I could put a date to – all I could see was Stephen
standing by the sink, washing dishes, or by the oven, cooking.

"How would I know?"

"You're his father. You could ask."

I should make allowances. Warren probably wasn't a parent.
He said, "Why do you suppose he changed the book?"

It wasn't a real question. He had offered tea, and now he
was going to lecture me.

"So I couldn't read it anymore?"

"So you *would* read it," Warren replied, tucking a ballpoint
pen into the pocket of his lab coat.

The coat reminded me that I should go to the pharmacy.
Butler's moisturiser was all very well – and kind of her – but
the itching, the *pain*, was now such that it was surely time for
more intensive intervention.

"Do you think so?" It was necessary to go through this.
There was no way round. He was doing me a favour, the price
of which would be the obligation to listen to my elder's sage
advice. I had no idea how old Warren was, but it was older
than me.

"To make you notice him again. You need to talk to your
son, Mr Exley. He is not happy."

Of course Stephen wasn't happy. Nobody was happy. Which was precisely why I didn't want to talk to him.

I folded the sheet of numbers into three, as if I were preparing to post it in a letter, and thrust it into my jacket pocket.

"I'll ask."

That evening, as if the conversation had never been interrupted, Leach said, "But what do you suppose she does?"

Since the night after the bad day that had ended in neat tequila and vomit, Butler hadn't come to the pub with us again. Since her day off sick and the conversation we'd had when she returned, about how she could not resign (the conversation in which I'd called her Brigid) she had not mentioned any of it again. The junior defence minister, his wife, their children and the nanny; the architect and her lawyer husband, with their suicide vests. They were all just as dead, of course, but Butler had not mentioned them. She hadn't mentioned the murderers' twin girls, either, who were now living with their mother's sister, and would grow up wondering whether their parents thought about them while they did what they did, and would have no better answers than any of us. She had returned to her duties, not as if nothing had happened, exactly, but as if what had happened had been dealt with. As if one drunken binge, one day sick, one conversation were enough for her: part of the task, duly completed.

And what was the task?

She had shown us she was human – although whether that made her more like us, or less was not obvious. Now she could carry on.

Was that unfair?

The fact was: she had carried on.

And Leach's question wasn't really a question, just resentment.

I said, "I expect she has a life."

He made a sour face.

We all have a life, of course. That's the problem.

"I picture her in a gym," Leach said, "Stretching on some weights machine, thighs spread, arms spread, mouth open, a trickle of sweat . . ."

"She's right - you're a pig."

Simmons returned from the bar with two pints and a glass of white wine.

Leach said, "Are you not drinking?"

Simmons pointed to her glass. Leach waited.

"Nick's lumbered us with some dinner party tonight. I can't turn up stinking of beer."

I said, "Nick?"

"My husband."

I couldn't remember her mentioning her husband's name before. "Not Nicola, then?"

"Nicola doesn't do dinner parties. She does sleepovers. Only now they involve Jägerbombs and poppers."

Leach said, "Your husband's Nick and your daughter's Nicola?"

"It was his mother's idea."

We sipped our drinks.

Simmons turned to Leach. "How about you? Any family revelations to declare?"

"I'm married to the job," Leach said, straight-faced.

"It's probably cheating on you with your best friend. Oh, wait. You don't have any friends."

"But you're my friends." Leach smirked, his voice sickly.

An image of Gibbon's office popped uninvited into my mind.

I said, "That file you passed me?"

Simmons looked instinctively from side to side: this wasn't the place.

"Crock of shit," I said.

She looked relieved. "Good. I mean, thanks."

She left earlier than usual, for her dinner party, she said.

"Who has dinner parties?" Leach said gloomily when she'd gone. "Especially on a weeknight?"

It was Friday.

We thought about our weekends for a while.

I would go to the supermarket in the morning. Stephen was probably writing out the shopping list for me already. We would share a pork pie for lunch. Maybe a tin of soup, given how cold it was. Stephen would go to his cello lesson. He rarely played these days. He still went to lessons every week, though, manhandling his cello case to the station and through a change of trains to get there. Or perhaps he didn't? Perhaps he just pocketed the money I gave him for lessons and spent a couple of hours every weekend in a life of his own? I'd never know. Going to the cinema alone, drifting through the shops, stretching time in cafes. Measuring out his life in coffee spoons, Mary used to say, in that way she had that meant it was something people said.

It was what I'd have done at his age.

A cello, though? Lugging a cello around seemed like pretty cumbersome tradecraft.

On Sunday, he would work. He'd have an essay to write, a passage of Sophocles to translate, a poem to parse. I would cook for once, and we'd come together in the early evening, a gin for me, a Coke for Stephen, a bowl of nuts. I'd offered Stephen gin, but he didn't like it. He'd have a glass of wine with dinner. He was seventeen and that was all he ever drank, which seemed to me both right and utterly wrong. Afterwards, he'd help me wash the dishes before going upstairs to write his journal and go to bed. I would iron our shirts and polish our shoes. Stephen had offered more than once, but I hated ironing and thought that would be a step too far.

The weekend would be over.

To Leach I said, "I'm on duty."

It was a thoughtless lie. I only wanted to head off any questions about my plans for the weekend, but there was a one in three chance I'd be immediately exposed.

"No you're not. I am."

Shit.

"I must have got confused. Want to swap?"

A stupid lie that now meant I was going to be on weekend duty after all.

I nodded at Leach's almost empty glass, bought another round.

# THAT'S NOT WHY I ASK

WHENIWOKEUP THE MORNINGAFTERDAD-
DIDN'TMAKEIT homeatall, the housewasempty. I
skipped breakfast but wasstilllateforschool. Xwinkedwhen I
came in halfwaythroughGreek and Hawkinsstartedbollock-
ingme. I'm prettysure she winked. It won't helpmychances of
getting to playOrestes, though. Of being her brother, or her
son (and killer). Plus I was starvingall morning.

Tonighhtwhen Dad came in, I askedhimhow his night had
been.

I always ask abouthis day. It startedas a joke – because
sometimes I feel like I'm his wife, cookinghis dinner and
warming his slippers by the fire, and because sometimes if I
don't speak he won't say anything at all, just drift up to his
room to change out of his suit and drift back down to eat
whatever it is I've cooked. He treats the place like a hotel.
Anyway, he never seems to get the joke and now it's become
a habit I can't really drop. I ask about his day at work and he
doesn't tell me much; he asks about my day at school and I
don't say much. At least we're talking.

So when I asked, this evening, how his night had been,
meaning the night he hadn't come home, I don't think he
heard the change, because he doesn't really listen, or need to,
normally.

He said what he always says, *viz*: "If I told you that, I'd
have to kill you." I think he says this because (a) it makes him

sound like he's dealing with ultra-secret spy-stuff even while he's cool enough to know he has to make a joke about dealing with ultra-secret spy stuff; and (b) it means he doesn't have to actually tell me anything. Which I wish he'd realize is okay, that I don't mind. I don't actually want to know the details of his working day. Except then it would be impossible to ask and we wouldn't have anything at all to say, instead of just not much.

So I said, "Busy night?"

He said there'd been bomb threats at the railway stations and I must have heard it on the news.

I didn't ask him why he didn't phone. I mean, I know they have rules and they're the only people in the world who don't have mobile phones, but if he was stuck at work it's not like there isn't a phone on his desk. He could have called. I didn't ask.

He said these things went with the job, sometimes.

I didn't ask him where he'd spent the night, or say that from the state of him it must have been: *in a fucking ditch*.

He said I wouldn't want a dad who worked nine-to-five in an insurance office, would I?

This was almost a joke because he knew I knew insurance is their cover. It's what they're supposed to say when anyone asks what they do, although Dad doesn't. He says: if I told you that, I'd have to kill you.

I didn't ask because I'm not in fact his wife, and not his mother, and if he told me he'd spent the night shagging his secretary, if he has a secretary, he really would have to kill me. Or watch me kill myself.

I don't want to know.

That's not why I ask.

That's why I didn't ask.

# I'M FINE

W HEN LEACH LEFT to catch his train I decided I would make the walk home we'd all been too drunk to make earlier in the week, the night of the bomb scare. All except Butler.

Five miles. An hour and a half, maybe. It would do me good. It might help the itching.

It was cold outside; a raw December city cold that was five parts damp to three parts poverty and depression. I had a coat, though, and the walk would keep me warm.

The pavements around the station were crowded with suited men and women dragging themselves underground while brighter, louder, more vivid specimens spewed out towards the bars and clubs. Newspaper hawkers split bundles and hawked their wares, even though the papers were free. The headlines trumpeted peace talks somewhere that hadn't seen peace for decades and probably wouldn't for decades more.

I slipped through the crush, against the tide, heading away from both crowds, following a busy four-lane road clogged with diesel traffic and despatch riders. The air was thick enough to chew. The muted glare of headlamps smeared across the glossy skins of stationary cars and petered out in the fine, suspended drizzle. Each streetlamp supported its own halo. As I headed south, the pavements quickly emptied, and I could pick up a proper walking pace. I found myself measuring my stride against the cracks between the paving stones – two steps, three slabs; two steps, three slabs – something I hadn't done since I was Stephen's age, or probably younger.

He would have cooked by now. Walking would make me later than usual, but it didn't matter. Whatever he'd cooked I could reheat when I got home. I wondered why he'd changed the source book for his journal code again so soon after the last time. Warren's logic – that he changed it to make sure I was paying attention – was sound enough. But why now? I hadn't gone home the night before he changed it – the night I hadn't walked – but that didn't seem much of a reason. There'd been other incidents, other emergencies, mostly no more real, other nights I hadn't made it home. It was the nature of the job. Stephen knew that. More likely he was approaching some sort of denouement in the Christmas panto, or whatever it was he had my father acting out.

After a mile or so I realized I was sweating. Despite the cold, despite the penetrating damp, my woollen coat was far too heavy for exercise. I took it off and slung it over my shoulder, but the dragging weight cut off the circulation in my fingers and the posture left me cramped. I tried draping the coat over my forearm, but that just made walking awkward. I switched hands, switched shoulders. I loosened my collar and pulled out my shirttails. Still sweat trickled into my body's cracks and crevices, soaked into the seams of my clothing. My heavy suit trousers chafed uncomfortably against the patches of dry skin on my thighs and hips. Pain – much more than an itch – began to stab at my anus.

Moisturiser was beside the point.

But moisturiser had been one of the things I'd found in Gibbon's office. There'd been other things, of course. An empty in-tray, an out-tray with nothing to go but a month-old journal, a ticked-off circulation list stapled to the cover. The list included Gibbon's initials. A cupboard mostly full of files, except for the bottle of whisky, a decanter of port and a set of old-fashioned cut-glass tumblers. Nothing I wouldn't have expected – nothing I hadn't seen the last and only other time I'd been in there, when Mary died and it had been Gibbon's predecessor's office. There was only one real change that I could see. On the wall opposite the desk there'd been an eighteenth-century fox hunting print: bright red-coated gentlemen cleared hedges on stiff-legged horses, or tumbled into ditches while the hounds swirled past like a disease. It had been replaced by a much larger print of a group portrait. As I sat in Gibbon's chair, a dozen pairs of eyes gazed back at me from a dark and gloomy palace room, the high walls panelled and covered with paintings. To the left, a painter leaned back, brush and palette in hand, a red cross like a dagger wound on his black tunic, contemplating his canvass, of which only the back was visible. A gaggle of servants, clerics, dwarves and a dog gathered around a young blonde child, a princess, tricked out in full hooped gown and floral decorations, who gazed out with innocent apprehension: desire, perhaps, for approval. Behind them all, at the back of the room, a door stood open and on the steps behind, framed in brighter light, right foot a step higher than the left, a courtier waited to lead us away, out through the labyrinthine palace corridors. To the left of the doorway, above and behind the princess's head, hung a mirror. And in the mirror, which was placed precisely to reflect the point from which a viewer might observe the painting, the point at which the painter, the courtier, the princess and her servants all stared, expectantly, the point just behind the desk in which I sat, gazing up at the picture on Gibbon's office wall, I could just make out the reflection not of myself, of course, not of Gibbon, but of two figures, a man and a woman I would later discover to be King Philip IV of Spain and his Austrian wife, Mariana. The moisturiser was in Gibbon's desk drawer, along with the usual clutter of dried-up marker pens and bulldog clips and perished rubber bands. The same brand of moisturiser that Butler had given me.

Two steps; three paving stones.

What would Butler be doing now? She'd left earlier than the rest of us, zipping up her bright yellow reflective cycling jacket and carrying her folding bike to the lift. Perhaps Leach was right, and she was in a gym. Perhaps she was at home, preparing supper with friends or a lover. Or perhaps she hadn't left at all? Just taken the lift to another floor?

This part of the walk was dark, darker than the rest. The road was broad, the streetlamps set back amongst trees that obscured their light even now, in December, when there were no leaves. The sparse traffic passed rapidly; there was nothing here to linger for. To my right, across the road, a long, unbroken terrace of flat-fronted townhouses, each divided into half a dozen bedsits, leaned back from narrow gardens full of wheelie bins big enough to contain a couple of corpses. Some of the windows were lit, the curtains still undrawn. I could see lampshades, pictures against wallpaper, stained ceiling plaster. A woman with a veil in a third floor window disappeared from view as she pulled the string and let drop a thin cotton blind. To my left, a vast brutalist estate sat back from the road behind a wall topped with rusty iron fencing. Blocks of flats like huge predatory animals squared off against each other, motionless but apparently alert, awaiting any sign of weakness.

The flanks of each block were marked with horizontal streaks of yellow light where dimly lit walkways led past door after door after door, all closed.

The wrong flat.

When I'd asked the man from Operations what that could possibly mean, given that the flat they'd raided had been stuffed with knives and guns and explosives and money, the man from Operations didn't know. He was just liaison. He would talk to the Team Leader, he said. He would get back to me on Monday.

There was a bus shelter a few yards ahead of me now. Its illuminated advert glowed like a synthetic oasis. Two men in puff-padded jackets and low-slung jeans leaned against a gigantic woman's face, her skin moisturised to peach perfection. As I approached, they turned to look at me, taking in the coat slung over my shoulder, the open collar, the un-tucked shirt. One of them stamped his feet and blew on his hands, rubbing them together in a pantomime of winter chill. He said, "You hot, boss?"

Not slowing down, not meeting the man's eye, I said, "I'm fine."

"He's fine," the second man mimicked.

"He's pissed."

"He's on something."

As they spoke, the two men stepped away to either side of the advertising hoarding, blocking my passage.

"So what are you on?"

"I'm fine."

"What have you got?"

"What are you going to share?"

One of them, the one who'd spoken first, stepped up to

me, threw an arm around my shoulder. "It's nearly Christmas, boss. You got a present for us?"

I shrugged off his arm. Now that it was too late not to, I looked him in the eye.

"I'm fine."

The next move was predictable. I wasn't in Operations, never had been, but we'd all done the same initial training, all gone through the same refresher courses. As the man's knee rose towards my groin, I dropped my coat and chopped down with my forearm, deflecting the impact and tipping him off balance. Before he could recover, I caught the still-raised leg, stepped through and dumped him on the pavement, stamping on the fingers of his right hand for good measure. The second man swung a wide, round punch at my head. I caught it, twisted the arm behind his back, and broke it. He howled in outrage, his face turning grey as pain overcame surprise. The first man came back up, a large ugly knife held awkwardly in his left hand. I took it off him, breaking a finger or two in the process, and lobbed it gently up onto the roof of the bus shelter. I slammed his nose into the advertising hoarding, cracking the screen and causing the woman with perfect skin to pixelate and ripple serenely like a pond in which a large, lazy fish has broken the surface. In the brief time the fight had taken, two or three cars had passed. None had stopped, or even slowed down.

When Stephen asked about my day, what would I say about this?

Nothing, obviously.

If I told him what I did I'd have to kill him.

I picked up my coat, brushed it down and continued walking. I found a phone box that, miraculously, contained a working telephone, and summoned an ambulance. It was nearly Christmas, after all. When the operator asked my name, I hung up. Rude, I dare say, but they're used to it.

I walked on towards home. The itching and the pain, the pain that seemed earlier to have shifted upwards, and inwards, to have become internal, as if it were a part of me, now seemed to have disappeared. I knew it would return, that its absence was just the effect of adrenaline. All the same, I did not pass the cherry tree, I did not think about the lottery.

WHEN EYQUEM WAKES up it is dark beneath the handkerchief that covers his face. Which doesn't mean much, he knows. At this time of year, this far north, it is dark most of the time. It might still be Christmas Day, or St Stephen's morning. When it is his shift, he can look out, like Wenceslas. There'll be no shortage of snow, though any peasant scavenging for firewood up here would be seriously lost.

Dark and very, very quiet.

Perhaps it is his shift, already, and he has overslept?

Surely Jacobs would have woken him?

Has he worked through the night? He has no memory of doing so, but that is obviously no guarantee. The job consists in looking out at mountains in the hope – always fulfilled – of seeing nothing. So it is hardly surprising that a shift, whole days, entire weeks and even months might pass without any distinguishing feature at all impressing itself on his mind and making it possible to recall what he had done or not done on any particular day, or whether, with any certainty, that day, that week, that month, has passed or not.

But yesterday was not like that.

Yesterday was Christmas Day.

Yesterday Our Lord was born. Humankind had been saved, again.

Yesterday – if it was yesterday, and not still today – had not been a success.

Once Cable was out of his bin and pouring whisky from the second demijohn there had been no going back. Eyquem knew it was a losing cause. He said his lines, Jacobs his, with heavy prompting. Brooks tried to contribute to the spirit of the thing, demanding his pap with creditable impatience. But Cable kept up a running fire of sarcastic commentary, like a guerrilla harassing regular troops from the safety of the surrounding mountainside. *What was it about, then? What was it supposed to mean?*

Eyquem said that wasn't the point.

*What was the point?*

The point was . . . the point was to perform. To be doing something. Instead of nothing.

*Sitting in a bin?*

They would be performing sitting in a bin.

They carried on as best they could.

But when, in character, and entirely according to the script, Eyquem found himself asking if they might perhaps be beginning to *mean something*, it was all up.

What had happened after that?

There'd been whisky, Eyquem knows, and the bottle of vile wine he'd brought up from the village himself, plundered from the reverend's inadequate cellar by Rachel Slater and slipped into one of his bags. There had been food. There had been songs. Singing and shouting and dominoes – *dominoes!* – and, he is almost certain, Cable smashing Brooks' ukulele and Brooks proving to be not quite so accommodating after all. There had been fighting, and more shouting and blood – he is sure there had been blood, although less sure whose. His own? It is not impossible. The handkerchief over his face even now seems to be stained with it – with blood, and whisky.

And then what?

What?

And then, after that, after the fighting, and the ukulele, he is almost certain, they quietened down, Cable quietened down, it was possible he slept, and Eyquem had suggested they have another go at the play.

Or was that before the ukulele and the blood?

Perhaps.

Now, though, it is quiet.

Perhaps if he removes the handkerchief?

When he tries to move his hands, however – first his right, because he is right-handed; and then, when that does not work, his left – when he tries simply to *lift* the linen square from his face, he finds that neither of his hands will move; he discovers, what's more, that the effort of trying to move them causes sharp pains to shoot up the muscles of each arm in turn. He decides instead to blow the handkerchief clear of his face. As he fills his lungs, like a child preparing to extinguish eight, ten, twelve candles with a single blow, he feels something solid slide from his chest onto the bare mattress beside him. Interesting. He will investigate that later, when the handkerchief is gone. He blows. But the handkerchief, heavy and stiff with dried blood, or what might have been dried blood, will not lift clear.

He tries again, but not before twisting his head until one cheek lies flat upon the mattress. The handkerchief refuses to budge. He thrashes his head from side to side – his arms pinioned to his right and left, his legs, he now discovers, also trapped, stretched out together – until at last the solid, crusted linen carapace falls away, like a sloughed snakeskin, or the death mask of a violent, alcoholic saint.

Apparently it is not dark after all.

In the effort, the writhing and thrashing against whatever restrains him, the heavy object – whatever *that* is – has worked its way beneath him, between his body and the grey, stained mattress. He can feel it now against his back, cold even through his underwear.

His underwear.

Where is his shirt? Where, for that matter, are his waistcoat and the heavy, brocaded dressing gown that rightfully belongs to the Reverend Slater that he had been wearing for the play? Where are his trousers?

"Jacobs?"

He wonders why he has not thought to ask for help, or at least for an explanation, before now.

"Jacobs?"

It has been so quiet. That's why.

"Brooks? Cable?"

No one's there. Or else they're keeping schtum. It seems more likely there is no one there. From his vantage point in the bed in the northeastern corner, by twisting his neck as far to the right as it will go, he can see most of the hut. He has to admit, the corner position has this advantage. If the bed were under the window, his blind spot would be that much larger. It is still possible someone is hiding under the bed, perhaps, or crouched behind the chesterfield – taking great care to remain silent and out of sight. On the whole, however, it seems improbable.

But, if not here, where are they?

On the table he can see the hourglass, its upper bulb empty, the lower filled with turquoise sand. Jacobs should be checking for signals now, coming back any moment to turn the hourglass over. Perhaps that's where he is: outside, scanning the mountains, getting a little fresh air while he makes his anti-clockwise circuit after so long cooped up in the hut. Eyquem would happily overlook his partner's anti-clockwise preference – what difference, after all, does it make? – if only he were to come in now, rubbing his hands together and stamping his feet.

Unless it *is* his shift, Eyquem's shift, and *he* should be checking for signals?

He's in the bed, which only happens during Jacobs' shifts, and Jacobs isn't there.

It is snowing outside.

He can see snow through the south window and, turning his head, through the west window, where the sky looks darker and more threatening. The flakes – small, hard, insistent – fall steadily, like time, burying everything. Jacobs will not be outside in this weather. But he's not inside, either.

Only now does it occur to Eyquem to investigate the immobility of his arms and legs. In truth, there is little mystery, once he turns his head to look. He is lashed to the iron bed frame at the wrists and the ankles, tied with the thin ropes Cable had used to attach the whisky bottles to his bicycle. Arms outspread, legs together: not spread-eagled, then, but cruciform, a horizontal Christ in ragged grey combinations.

The solid, heavy object pressing into his back has been warmed by contact with his body and is no longer cold. Eyquem twists his torso as far to the left as his bonds allow, towards the eastern wall, and then repeatedly scoots back and forth, trying to sweep the object out, to edge it into daylight, until there – yes, there! – the tip emerges: pale, yellow, smooth, like bone, or horn.

Jacobs' hunting knife!

The knife had been on his chest when he awoke. It was only his own foolish movements that had caused it to slip onto the bed and beneath his back.

Jacobs has left him his knife.

(It seems clear to Eyquem now that Jacobs has left, that he is not outside, checking the views, or inside, under the bed, say, keeping very quiet.)

Jacobs has left him the knife, presumably to help him free himself now that Jacobs (and Cable? And Brooks?) have made their escape.

Escape from what?

It is possible that it was not Jacobs, but Cable or – more likely, Eyquem thinks – Brooks who left the knife, but how would either of them have known about it? Or have persuaded Cable to leave it behind?

None of this matters, now. What matters is that he has the knife, or rather that the knife is there, although he cannot reach it. Even if he had not moved, if the knife, with its blade folded into the ram's horn handle, still lay upon his chest where Jacobs – or Cable, or Brooks – had left it, what use would that be?

Perhaps they'd left it as a sign, a promise that one of them would return and cut him free?

Or a sign that one of them – Cable? Not Jacobs, not Brooks, surely? – would return to slit his throat?

Eyquem closes his eyes happily. Either way, there is nothing he can do.

I KNEW WHAT I WOULD DO

ESCHYLUS, APPARENTLY. *THE Oresteia.*
I never asked, despite my promise, but that's what I found on Stephen's desk, beside the typewriter, on Saturday afternoon while Stephen was at his cello lesson.

Another Penguin Classic: black, with a picture on the cover, the credits said, of a Mycenaean gold cup depicting the capture of a wild bull. To be honest, I couldn't see it. I'd never read the plays, or seen them. I thumbed past the introduction to the first page of the script and read:

> And now I watch for the light, the signal fire
> breaking out of Troy, shouting Troy is taken.
> So she commands, full of her high hopes.

I had no idea who she might be, but I knew this was it. Stephen's new source.

I checked and memorized the translator's name and the publication date, then replaced the book exactly as I'd found it, left of the typewriter at an angle of thirty degrees to the edge of the desk.

"Could be haemorrhoids," the pharmacist had said brightly, that morning.

My heart sank. Like most people, I suspect, I have always welcomed illness, but would prefer it to be serious, even life-threatening, to absolve me from choice and responsibility. Having haemorrhoids was a complaint I'd have to live with, not one to which I could succumb.

"Or it might be colorectal cancer. Is there any bleeding?" She was a cheerful young woman, not long out of college, I guessed, and eager to help.

I said there wasn't, or hadn't been, yet, but honestly I didn't know. I couldn't say I'd looked.

She told me I should and, before handing over a tube of ointment, made me agree to consult my doctor if the condition got no better, or if there was any blood in my stool.

Leaving the pharmacy, I thought: *stool* was such an odd word. A ridiculous word.

Cancer, on the other hand, was a word to be reckoned with.

Mary smoked; I never did. I never liked the taste, or the smell, except on Mary.

Stephen's list specified partridges, but in the butcher's shop the Saturday boy with the haircut of a marine and the cheerless demeanour of a Victorian rat-catcher said they had sold out. I assumed this was a euphemism for not knowing what I was talking about. Did I want a pheasant?

I stuck with chicken. I knew what I would do with a chicken. Stephen had also stipulated preserved lemons – though where he thought I'd find them, even if I knew what I'd be looking for, was anybody's guess. I'd roast a chicken and some potatoes. I'd make bread and butter pudding. We both liked bread and butter pudding. Mary had, too.

On Sunday afternoon, while I was cooking, and Stephen was upstairs – reading Aeschylus, I presumed – the telephone rang. I swore at the sound. I wouldn't normally bother answering, but remembered just in time that I'd swapped duty rotas with Leach. A woman's voice asked me to identify myself and, once I'd given the correct day code, put me through to a man who did not identify himself.

"Sorry to bother you at the weekend, Exley," he said in a voice buttery with rounded vowels. "Only, we were hoping you might be able to help clear up a little matter for us."

I waited. There was no point trying to guess what he was talking about, even if I wanted to.

"We've had a couple of chaps turn up in A&E on Friday night – broken arm, broken nose, couple of broken fingers: nothing life-threatening. But, the thing is, they're ... connected, and wouldn't say how they got there. Disappeared as soon as the morphine wore off."

"Connected?"

"Not on the payroll but ... contractors we sometimes use."

That made some sense. They'd been far too clumsy for professionals.

"Thing is, Exley, it was your neck of the woods. And *we* thought" – he stressed the *we*, seeking to imply that everyone from the Director-General down had considered this, and was in agreement – "that is, we wondered, if you might just be aware of any Ops that could have been underway but not, you know, on the books?"

"Who did you say you were, sir?"

I threw in the 'sir' to soften the challenge, and maybe confuse the man a little. He was obviously an underling, albeit an underling to important people.

"I didn't."

Neither of us said anything for a while.

"Exley?"

"I am not aware of any unofficial operations taking place on Friday, sir."

"You're not aware?"

"How could I be? If they weren't official?"

Another, briefer silence.

"You hadn't ordered anything?"

"Of course not, sir."

"Of course not."

I left a beat.

"If I had ordered anything, it would have been official, wouldn't it? Sir."

The voice, oleaginous as ever, thanked me insincerely, wished me a pleasant remainder of the weekend, and hung up.

I returned to the chicken. I sliced a lemon in two – an ordinary lemon, preserved only with carcinogenic pesticides – and squeezed one half over the carcass. He was fifth floor, by the sound of the vowels; or, more likely, one of their epigones. Why had I given him such a run around? It would only heighten their suspicion. I sucked my finger where lemon juice cauterized a cut I hadn't noticed before. Of course, I hadn't wanted the conversation to lead anywhere near why I'd hospitalized two operatives, amateur or otherwise. It wasn't something I was proud of, or from which I could extricate myself without effort. But I could have just said "No" politely, couldn't I?

No, I knew nothing.

Couldn't I?

Now I'd gone and made them think I knew something. Something I was letting them know I knew. When, in reality, I knew nothing. They wouldn't let that go. Whoever they were.

Christ. Wasn't the whole point of cultivating indifference to avoid this kind of aggravation?

I stuffed the other half lemon up the chicken's arse and slammed it in the oven.

Back in the office on Monday, I took another call from Operations, from the Team Leader, a down-to-earth woman with a rasp in her voice that sounded like cigarettes and sex. I was pretty sure I knew her – we'd worked together before – although of course she did not give her name.

It was the wrong flat, she said, because there'd been some dispute amongst the wazzocks – her word – in her team as to whether the third floor was actually the fourth floor – that is, the third floor above the ground floor – or the third floor from the ground.

She blamed the Americans for this, she said, as for so much else.

They had raided the wrong flat, the flat directly below the flat intended. Which, I thought, at least explained why the neighbour on the TV news had referred to the occupants as a "family" while the surveillance reports had mentioned only an adult man, an adult woman, and a number of more or less unsavoury visitors.

And yet it had been the right flat, in that it contained, alongside the unexpected family, exactly what we're always looking for: a bomb factory, an arsenal and a mountain of cash. Exactly what, if this were indeed Scenario 4, someone wanted me to find. But could that someone conceivably have factored in the random incompetence of Operations? Could anyone have predicted not only their ability to raid the wrong flat – admittedly, a fair bet, given the historical precedents

- but precisely *which* wrong flat? That seemed unlikely.

But wasn't it equally unlikely that Ops had simply stumbled on a genuine terrorist operation by purest happenstance?

Either way, the question remained: what had been going on – what might still be going on – in the flat above? The flat I'd actually ordered them to raid? Now I thought about it, hadn't the neighbour on the TV news said she lived in the flat above? I couldn't be sure: I would have to check the archive.

I had to stand up, anyway. The itching – the pain – was becoming too much to bear.

The surveillance report had described the woman in the target flat as short, and blonde, which wasn't much to go on. It said she wore a pale blue raincoat, which might be more helpful unless the weather changed, and that she had once gone out in her slippers. The woman on the TV news, when I recovered the clip, was wearing a skirt that stopped some way short of her bare knees and a leather jacket. No raincoat; no slippers. But her hair was blonde and when I froze the clip and compared her image to that in the surveillance report it certainly looked like the same woman.

Which proved nothing, of course, other than that she lived in the flat she said she lived in. The flat Operations should have raided. But if her own flat were full of plastic explosives, what was she doing in front of the cameras, giving character references for the benefit of passing journalists?

Which meant either there was nothing in her flat, or that there was, but she didn't know. Or, just possibly, that there was, she knew it, and was hiding in plain sight. I played the clip again. It was hard to say. The lighting was poor and the editing cut away from her abruptly, but to me it now looked as if, just as she finished saying what a lovely family her neighbours were – no trouble, no noise, always ready to help you out – as if – and surely this could not be possible? – as if she winked at the camera, at me.

It wasn't possible.

But that's what I saw each time I replayed the clip.

So she commands, I thought, full of her high hopes.

T HE COLD WOULD have killed him.
   When she found him – more dead than alive, she says, later, when it seemed to Eyquem that he was neither – even before cutting through the ropes, she piled his ancient great-coat, her own thick beaver-pelt fur, and all the rugs and blankets she could find on top of the bed, on top of him. She crept beneath the pile herself to lie over his corpse, belly-to-belly, face-to-face, pulling the coats over their heads and hoping – praying, even – that the warmth of her breath and of her body would bring him back to life.

It was New Year's Day, she says, though he does not believe it. Surely that would be too trite, too convenient?

The stove had been out for a week.

There was ice, Rachel says, in his beard, where a thin stream of drool had trickled from his open mouth, and frozen. The blood on his wrists and ankles had frozen, too.

"It was New Year's Day," she says. "He threw me out on New Year's Eve."

She doesn't say why. Eyquem doesn't ask, but he can guess, which is why he doesn't ask.

No one would have checked the signals for a week.

She'd thought at once of Eyquem, she says, of his kindness, his mildness, of the way he had once reached up and stroked her cheek. That time beneath the beech tree.

Does he remember?

She came straight here, she says, walking through the night. He wonders how she knew the way, in the dark, in the snow. The path must have been buried; she has never been here before. She just kept climbing, she says, making each step higher than the last, knowing that must, in the end, bring her here.

Once she was sure it was safe to leave the bed, that he would not die, she cleaned out the cold ash and re-lit the stove. She cut the ropes that bound him to the bed with the knife she found beneath his frozen body. She melted snow to wash his wounds and feed him, a drop at a time, between his cracked lips. She made porridge, stirring in thick molasses. Even so it had been a day, and a night, she says, before he could speak.

He asks if she has seen Jacobs – or Brooks, or Cable – or any sign of them. It was dark, she says, and the snow was thick and falling heavily when she arrived.

They are alone.

He asks her to look out of the windows – he is still too weak to stand. Start with the east window, he says, and go clockwise around the hut.

"What am I looking for?"

"A sign."

She laughs.

"A beacon," he says. "Fire on the mountains."

"And what should I do if I see one?"

"Light our beacon."

"And then?"

And then, he says, they would have to see.

When she has looked out of each window and reported jauntily back – "Nothing to see, sir!" – he asks her to turn the hourglass on the table in the middle of the room.

She turns it over. She tells him the sand is beautiful but she cannot watch it trickling through: it is too sad. He should not watch it, either, she says.

Over the next few days Eyquem observes how quickly the miraculous becomes routine. Rachel is not Jacobs. She checks the windows willingly, even cheerfully. She keeps the stove alight; she makes coffee and porridge and feeds him, first tasting the food herself, making sure it is not too hot, then spooning it into his mouth. When he is well enough, he begins to take over, gradually building up his shifts until things are back to normal.

Not normal.

One day, about two weeks after her arrival, Rachel completes her circuit outside: the sun is shining although the temperature is well below freezing. She tramps around the hut, crunching through the frozen snow; she stamps her boots until they are clean, and returns, deliberately allowing a blast of icy, antiseptic air to stir the fetid atmosphere of the hut. She turns the hourglass over, kicks off her boots, drops her beaver coat to the floor, followed by her woollen dress, and, climbing in to bed, she says: "You've got thirty minutes, mister."

After that, each morning, each evening, as they change shifts, they make love.

A few weeks later – around the middle of February – when she has been on duty all night and now it is his turn, when she is lying with her arm across his chest, her leg across his thigh, she says: "Stay here. Don't get up."

"The hourglass is empty."

"Doesn't matter."

He holds her tighter for a moment. "You sound like Jacobs."

She rubs her thigh against his, gently flicks his penis with her hand. It stirs.

"Really?"

"No. Not really."

He stays in bed, but only for five minutes or so.

"Happy Valentine's Day," she says.

Later, looking out of the windows, especially looking south, he begins to see the change. Down in the valley, where the village is – with its pub, its store, and its vicar – the snow has already begun to melt. Soon there will be flowers: snow-drops, then crocuses. Lambs will be born and the Reverend Slater will welcome Lent.

Up on the mountain, the coffee runs out. The porridge will last a little longer, but, as soon as the thaw comes, one of them will have to go down for supplies.

"It comes in April."

This year will be no different. By the end of March, the insidious ticking will begin, as the snow on the roof starts imperceptibly to melt. It will slide down the icicles hanging from the eaves, then drip, drip, drip into the snow banked up against the walls. At first there will be some relief each evening as the sun drops behind the mountains and the melt re-freezes. But the sun will rise again – busy old fool, what choice does it have? – the temperature will rise, and the drips, the tick-tick-tick, incessant as any clock, as the trickle of sand in the hourglass, will begin again.

"You'll want to go then."

"Go where?"

Outside the landscape will creak and crack and, slowly, the barren ice will retreat to reveal barren rock.

"I don't know. Lourdes? Santiago de Compostela?"

Rachel laughs. "Why on earth would I want to do that?"

"It's the season for pilgrimage."

She hugs him from behind, pulling him closer. "I'm not a vicar's wife any more. Besides, vicars don't approve of pilgrimage. They approve of tea with seed cake and sermons on the need for moderation."

Somewhere, through four or five layers of clothing, he can feel her breasts pressing against his back. He is almost certain of it.

Inspiration strikes. "I'll have to go. You're not authorized to sign the Faculty's forms." He is afraid that if she leaves, she will never return. But she agrees; she does not want to go.

"Don't tell anyone I'm here."

"You'll be all right?"

"I'll be all right."

April is also the start of the fighting season. If ever there were to be a signal, that's when it would be.

"I'll be fine. You go. Just watch what you get up to while you're there."

She kisses him, scrapes traces of porridge from their bowls. "And bring us food that tastes of something. Meat. Smoked fish."

"Caviar?"

"You're teasing. Bring something to drink. Wine."

"Champagne?"

"Or whisky."

Eyquem thinks of Cable, standing in the open doorway on Christmas Eve. "Not whisky."

"Brandy, then. Something to keep us warm."

"It'll be summer before you know it."

The tick-tick-tick begins, followed by cracks and thuds

as the icicles break off and spear the snow. Finally, with a scraping, growling, rushing sound like a plough turning stony ground, great sheets of ice and snow shift, slip, then gather pace and cascade from the iron roof onto the ground behind the hut.

"Remember: fish, meat, brandy."

"Truffles, lark's tongues, Chateau d'Yquem."

It would be porridge, molasses and tinned sardines. Rice if they were lucky. Coffee that was more acorn than coffee. But he won't tell her that.

The bicycle is not where it's supposed to be, sheltered under the eastern eaves. As the thaw continues, though, they spot handlebars poking up through the retreating snow, twenty yards from the hut. They venture out to excavate, and uncover a corpse, rigid, one foot still tangled in the bicycle's chain.

"That's Brooks."

Eyquem looks a little closer. "That's Brooks' bicycle, too."

Of his bicycle – his and Jacobs' – there is no sign.

Rachel says, "Do you suppose the others made it?"

She has never ask about what happened, about Christmas and St Stephen's Day.

He shrugs.

He walks, clockwise, around the mountaintop, checking the views. When he returns to Rachel, she says: "What are we going to do with him?"

They can't bury him, not on the mountain. Even when the thaw is complete, there'll be nothing but rock.

"We could cremate him."

Eyquem considers the idea, shakes his head. "We'd have to chop him up to get him in the stove. I can't do that."

"We could build a pyre."

He turns to look at the beacon. They can't light it. They can't light a fire to burn Brooks. Not without a signal.

"I'll have to wheel him down to the valley."

It is easier said than done. They stand Brooks' bicycle against the hut and haul his corpse up onto it. They tie his feet to the pedals, his hands to the handlebars, using the ropes from Cable's whisky jars, the ropes she cut away from his own wrists and ankles. They tie a shovel to Brooks' back.

"Take care," she says, kissing him. "Hurry back."

"Keep watch while I'm gone."

He sets off, one hand under the back of the saddle, the other on the brake, touching Brooks' own cold hand. It is oddly intimate, as if Brooks were an overgrown child he is teaching, too late, to ride a bike. He hopes Brooks will not thaw too much before they reach the village.

When he returns the following night, Rachel is not in the hut. She can't have been gone long, or gone far. She has no bicycle; the stove is still burning. On the table in the centre of the hut, beside a lighted candle, sand still trickles through the hourglass.

She must be at the stream. He begins stacking bags of coffee, flour and rice – it has been a good haul, after all – in the hut's only cupboard. He hides the small bottle of brandy and the jar of Spanish olives with which he hopes to surprise her at the back, behind the flour.

When the sand runs out, she has not returned.

He goes out again, back into the night. The sky is ablaze with stars, the Milky Way a soft white blanket, like spring sheep's wool, stretched from mountain to mountain above his head. The ground at his feet gleams silver, as if still covered in ice. He walks clockwise around the hut, looking for signals, looking for Rachel.

"HAVE YOU NOTICED how people keep disappearing?"

I wondered for a moment if I were missing something, some operation I'd been excluded from, some unofficial activity of the sort the plummy voice on the telephone a few days earlier had alluded to, if that was why Warren and I were here, in a quiet corner of the canteen, not down in the Crypt. He could have been referring to Gibbon, but he said, "In your son's journal."

"You read it?"

I knew he read it. This wasn't the first time he'd taken it upon himself to comment.

"Avidly."

I said, "It's not really a journal these days, is it? More of a story. I wonder if he's not trying to write a novel."

Warren finished his tea and began picking at the rim of his Styrofoam cup. "Perhaps. But Eyquem is your father, isn't he?"

He had never before suggested that we leave the Crypt and go up to the canteen – I'd swear I'd never seen him outside his own domain – but this time, instead of handing over the latest instalment, he had taken off his white coat and hung it on a peg by the double corridor doors that stared back blankly, like the entrance to an Egyptian mausoleum.

"I need to thaw sometimes," he said, by way of explanation,

merely underlining the lack of explanation for why he'd never needed to before.

In the canteen we both gravitated towards the table furthest from any of our colleagues, without either of us having to suggest it.

Was Eyquem my father?

In a manner of speaking. My father had been a beacon keeper, had spent most of his adult life on top of one mountain or another watching for signals. The young wife Stephen's Eyquem left behind in the city was my mother; I was her unborn child. But had my father been attacked and abandoned by his colleagues? Had he been rescued and fallen in love with another woman? It was possible. Such things happened, of course, but mostly in fiction.

In retrospect, the more interesting question, perhaps, was why they happened in Stephen's fiction. Never mind my father, would Stephen have known what a patissier was? Or a beech tree? He read a lot of books.

In his early years in the mountains, my father wrote infrequent letters to my mother. When she died, I found them, unsorted, in a drawer otherwise full of bank statements, empty chequebooks and leaflets about life insurance. Like his diary, the letters were resolutely factual, a log of weather and changing seasons, of logistical arrangements and meals consumed. They contained only passing, oblique references to his postings and his colleagues, which would, in any event, have been restricted by the Faculty's obsessive secrecy. The beacon-keeper of the letters would not be surprised that a fig-tree brought forth figs, but might have been surprised that anyone thought it worth writing down. There'd been no reference to any woman other than my mother, but then there wouldn't, would there? If he wrote any letters in the later years, my mother had not kept them.

Were there patterns in the data I had failed to recognize? There was the knife. The knife was real.

Warren appeared to be expecting an answer to his question. I'd assumed it was rhetorical.

I said, "Less and less so. Stephen's version seems to be taking over."

"You need to talk to your son, Exley."

He leaned back as he said it, presumably to make his words appear less challenging; it felt more condescending. I said, "So you say."

"What have you told him about Mary?"

It was a shock to hear Mary's name. Of course, Warren would have known her – everyone in the Faculty knew her. They all knew what happened.

I said, "He was there."

"He would have been – what? Two?"

It was true. I'd been buckling Stephen into his buggy. He had been bored and a little grizzly, struggling against the straps, throwing his gloves to the ground. Otherwise, Mary might very well have been pushing him.

"He saw what happened."

"Did he know she was pregnant?"

Stephen had known, in the way that people – even toddlers – know, but had we ever talked to him about it? Mary might have.

If she hadn't been pregnant, if an earlier scan had not thrown up some question of a spinal abnormality, we would not have been in the hospital, all three of us, that morning. If the scan hadn't proved to be a false alarm, had the consultant

162

obstetrician not sent us on our way with the cheerful benediction that – provided Mary quit smoking – there was no reason to suppose she would not complete a perfectly normal pregnancy, and give birth to a happy, healthy daughter. The doctor bit her lip, then. Had we been told the baby was a girl? We had. "She'll be a playmate for you, won't she?" the doctor said to Stephen, who refused to answer. "You'll be fine, Mrs Exley," she concluded, dismissing us. If she hadn't, if Stephen had not been grumbling as we left the hospital and had I not been trying to head off an incipient tantrum, Mary would not have been bounding ahead, floating almost, buoyed up by relief and happiness – despite everything she might have said, in other contexts, about indifference or the trouble with being born – and would not have stepped off the pavement in front of a bus that had no chance whatever of stopping before it hit her, crushed her, rolled over her and our unborn daughter both, and they would not have bled to death together on a bridge in the heart of the city, yards from the best, most sophisticated medical facilities anywhere in the world, which still made no difference whatsoever.

It wouldn't have happened.

But all of that – the chain of events, of doubt, fear, relief, happiness, carelessness and death – makes sense only if you accept that the world itself makes sense, however cruel and ugly. If there are causes and consequences, one thing leading to another until they end, like stories.

There is no end, no sense.

I said, "Stephen knew his mother was pregnant. He wanted a brother."

"He was two," Warren said again.

What difference did that make? I knew what he was

getting at. Stephen had been too young really to understand what death meant, what having a brother or a sister – not having a mother – might mean. The abrupt disappearances in Stephen's version of his grandfather's story were manifestations of Stephen's unresolved fears and sense of having been abandoned – betrayed – by his own family. Eyquem had not only abandoned his wife and son – abandoned me – but had been abandoned, and would of course, in Stephen's story, soon disappear himself. The journal was not a diary. Neither was it an experiment in style, a would-be novelist flexing his narrative muscles. It was an appeal for help, for reassurance from his father. That was the code Warren thought he had cracked.

I said, "People die. It's what they do."

"He was two."

"So you keep saying. I was twenty. So what?"

"Twenty?"

"When my father killed himself."

Warren swept up all the scraps of Styrofoam he had torn from his cup and dumped them into the puddle of cold tea in mine. "I'm sorry," he said. "It's not my business."

T HERE IS A fire, to the east, where the sky is deepest
black.

He does not see it at first. Or rather, he sees it, the point
of light flickers on his retina, but for a moment it signifies
nothing. This fire, this signal, for which he has waited so
long, which he has hoped all his life not to see, is there, on
the mountain, but his mind refuses to accept it.

He stands, gazing eastward, Rachel forgotten.

Nothing ever happens. That is the point of being a beacon
keeper: you keep watch; you do nothing. Now something is
happening. Now there is a signal. He has seen the signal and
he has a job to do. A task.

He returns to the hut. He takes a torch from the hooks on
the wall by the door and, opening the stove door, pushes it
inside. The pitch-soaked twigs begin to smoulder, to smoke
and then to spit. He pulls the torch out, burning fiercely now.
An acrid, chemical smell fills his nostrils: the scent of fire,
of humanity.

He carries the torch outside and thrusts it upwards into
the base of the beacon. It catches quickly and the smell of
burning pitch thickens, poisoning the mountain. Within
minutes the flames have spread from the bottom of the iron
basket to the highest branches of the pyre, a dozen feet above
his head. A plume of smoke rises higher still, grey against the
silver-black starlit night, rolling, growing, bursting like a thing

alive, like the army it heralds. He wonders if Cable has made it back. It is an idle thought; it does not matter. If he's not there, his partner – Burton? – will see Eyquem's signal. He will pass it on to whoever is further west, which is not the sea. The sea is further west than that, he is sure of it. Jacobs has not returned, Rachel has disappeared; that has not stopped Eyquem completing his task.

# BEER TIME

B ACK IN THE office I found the internal post had left a
new buff folder on my desk labelled "Volorik (?)".

The Faculty had long since given up on email, which was
hopelessly insecure. It had recreated a world of typewriters
and handwritten memoranda that none of us were old enough
to remember from the first time round. They'd banned mobile
phones, too. Gradually we reverted to a time before instant
communication, before office self-sufficiency, easy familiarity
and emotional incontinence. We stopped using given names.
There was no actual rule, no personnel procedure. No guid-
ance or instruction had been issued, but I would no more
address Simmons as Ellen – or Leach as Andrew – than I
would call them darling, or dickhead. (I had called Butler
Brigid.)

The folder contained the preliminary interrogation report
from last week's raid, the raid on the wrong flat. A man and a
woman had been questioned; two children – both boys, aged
five and seven – would have to be interviewed separately in
the presence of specialist operatives who, apparently, had not
been available to date.

The man gave his name as Konstantin Volorik, and provided a wealth of documentation to back up the claim, including
a US passport indicating that he had been born in Atlanta,
Georgia and was currently forty-two years old. A UK driving
licence. Utility bills, bank statements. Degree certificates from

Oxford and the Sorbonne. And a second, Irish, passport for good measure.

KV: *My grandmother was Irish.*

LI: *But you are American?*

KV: *I was born in America. I have lived in many places. My father came from the other Georgia, and we moved around a great deal.*

LI: *But you are a US citizen.*

*[Pause.]*

SI: *For the tape, please. You are a US citizen?*

KV: *Yes.*

LI: *And also an Irish citizen?*

KV: *I am large. I contain multitudes.*

*[Pause.]*

I imagined the Lead Interrogator looking at his colleague at this point, or at the one-way mirror on the wall, wondering what to make of that.

As the interrogation continued Volorik appeared polite, urbane, affable, and wholly un-intimidated. The woman, meanwhile – Julia Holland – agreed she was married to Konstantin Volorik, although she had not taken his name. (*"Would you?"*) She was British. She was the mother of the two boys.

An educated American/Irishman with a Georgian father, a British wife and two children he wasn't supposed to have. Would it have been possible to concoct a case more complicated – or with more diplomatic bear-traps for the Faculty? Perhaps if Julia Holland turned out to be a duchess?

I flipped through the transcripts and the report, knowing they would give me no hard facts, nothing incriminating or directly useful. They were character sketches, no more. How fictional the characters would turn out to be was a matter of conjecture.

Something caught my eye. Dear God, the woman really was a duchess. Well, a Viscountess. The daughter of a Viscount, anyway. I'd have to check what that made her. Viscount Holland had committed suicide twenty years earlier, when his predilection for cocaine and leather briefly caught the attention of the fourth estate. You couldn't make it up, I thought. Unless, of course, you had. Julia would have been a teenager at the time, still at school. About Stephen's age, in fact.

The report concluded that further interrogation would be required. Enhanced techniques might prove necessary, but no authorization was currently sought. I put it back in the folder and locked the folder in my desk drawer. Warren was wrong. It wasn't Stephen I really needed to talk to.

That evening, once Butler had donned her yellow jacket and left – her folding bike balanced heavily against one hip – but before the rest of us had packed up for the pub, I approached Simmons' desk.

"That case you passed on to me?" I spoke quietly, hoping Leach would not involve himself.

"The crock of shit?"

I nodded.

"How did it come to you?"

She shook her head, stuck out her lower lip. "In the internal post, I suppose. Along with half a dozen others."

"Was that before or after we last saw Gibbon?"

She raised her eyebrows, sighed, pondered. "After, I think. It's hard to say. Why?"

Her doubt could be real. Any day here was hard to

distinguish from any other. Or she could be lying. I decided to risk it. How much worse could my position get?

"Because something about it isn't right."

She laughed. "That hardly makes it unique."

I said nothing. How much should I reveal of what I knew? What did I know, really?

"You said it was a crock of shit."

"It is. It might be."

Leach was clearing his desk, obtrusively putting away his pens and papers and putting his jacket on. It was time to go to the pub.

"But it might not?"

I took a deep breath before the plunge.

"I think Butler is setting me up."

Instinctively, Simmons had absorbed my tone, speaking quietly, unemphatically. Conspiratorially. Now, surprised, she allowed her voice to rise.

"*Butler?*"

"She's gone," said Leach. "Beer time."

# A NEATER SOLUTION

H E HAS COMPLETED the task.

Eyquem returns to the hut. He opens the store cupboard and reaches for the brandy hidden there, dislodging a
bag of rye flour, which falls to the floor and bursts. He leaves
it there. He opens two tins of sardines and lines up the fish
along the griddle plate of the stove, where they hiss and spit
in their own oil. He cuts thick slices of bread and puts on a
pan of water to make coffee, the almost real coffee he carried
up from the village only an hour ago.

While the fish cook and the water boils, Eyquem picks
up the hourglass. Holding it by the empty end, he strikes the
heavy, sand-filled bulb against the edge of the table. It shatters,
spraying shards of broken glass and turquoise sand all over
the table and the floor around it. He throws the empty, intact
bulb against the wall, where it, too, shatters.

He eats the fish and drinks the coffee, followed by the
bottle of brandy. He falls asleep at the table, his head on his
arms.

He sleeps for fourteen hours.

When he wakes he can't remember dreaming. The stove
has gone out. He takes the birch twig broom and sweeps the
broken glass, the flour and the turquoise sand into a dustpan.
He carries it outside and empties it in one of the bins – Cable's
bin: the bin Cable had refused to stay in. Flour and sand
trickle down through layers of empty tins and paper sacks. The

171

beacon is still burning, though less vigorously now, the logs and branches fused into a single, intense core, like a collapsed star. No smoke stains the blue, still sky.

The beacon to the east has died; that to the west burns brightly.

Eyquem returns to the hut. He sweeps the cold ash out of the stove and begins to lay kindling, but stops, leaving it unlit. He walks over to the bed and pulls out the wooden box beneath it. He lifts the lid and rummages through the contents until he finds Jacobs' hunting knife. He takes the knife and goes back outside. He tries to sit cross-legged on the ground, but he is stiff from his journey back up the mountain and from sleeping in a chair, and it is too uncomfortable. He returns to the hut and pushes and shoves the chesterfield to the door, where it becomes wedged. It is far too large to go through. How had it got there in the first place? He cannot manage this alone.

He gives up and drags the chesterfield back indoors, catching and ripping the fabric against the hasp of the door's bolt. It doesn't matter. The sofa is old, and already very worn. He picks up one of the plain wooden chairs instead, then thinks again. A neater solution occurs to him.

He goes outside and picks up the empty bin – Brooks' bin, not Cable's – and carries it to the western side of the hut. He searches the rocky ground for space level enough to keep the bin stable, and climbs inside. Looking out, his head just above the rim, he can see the mountains in the clear spring afternoon, Cable and Burton's beacon burning, still, a plume of smoke rising gently, dispersing slowly in the barely moving air, like a crowd unwilling to accept the show is really over.

He climbs out again, and carries the bin around to the

south, from where he can see down towards the valley, to where the village must lie, hidden in the folding foothills, to where he knows – thanks to Rachel and their walks by the river – daffodils and magnolia, hyacinth and primrose will be flowering. He clambers back into the bin, his knees pushed up awkwardly, almost level with his shoulders. With some difficulty in the cramped space he undoes the buttons of his jacket and his waistcoat. He undoes his belt and loosens his trousers, tugs up his grey, unwashed shirt, his undershirt and his vests until his belly is exposed, white and gently rounded like the belly of a fish. He unfolds Jacobs' knife and, holding his clothes clear with his left hand, presses the tip of the tooled blade into the dimple just above his hipbone with his right. He feels the resistance of the flesh until, with a sudden release of tension, the skin splits and the blade penetrates the muscle. Blood wells in the wound as he tugs and hacks the blade from left to right, hip to hip below his navel. By the time the pain becomes too great and he drops the knife, his intestines are slipping from the wound and pooling, like lazy snakes, around his groin and on the cold metal base of the dustbin.

# FOUR OR FIVE YEARS LATER

# ONE

I T WAS FROM the Director-General that I first heard the word *seppuku*. Like most people in this country, I imagine, I was familiar with the term *harakiri*, although if I were honest I'd have to say I had only the vaguest notion of what it entailed. The existence of the practice was one of those facts – or rather one of the vast undifferentiated hodgepodge of half-truths and lies – one acquires about the world, and bears through life, without ever knowing how or why. He explained to me that the meaning of the two words is the same – both refer not only to ritual suicide, he said, but specifically to disembowelling oneself: cutting the belly (*seppuku*) or belly-cutting (*harakiri*). The difference arises from Chinese and Japanese readings of the characters for 'cut' and 'belly', and the reversal of their order. The Japanese, he said, tend to use the Chinese form *seppuku* in writing and more formal conversation to refer to what was, after all, a highly stylized performance.

I baulked at the word 'performance', and he admonished me gently. "What else would you call it?"

This conversation must have occurred shortly after we first met – that is, sometime after Stephen wrote about his grand-father's death, finished school and left home for university, from which he has now returned. It would have taken place in a room three or four floors below ground level, below the Crypt, below anything I had known existed. I didn't know it was possible to go down so far.

That morning I had received a meeting request – or rather an instruction – in a memorandum signed 'B', summoning me from my own office to another, much larger office on the fifth floor – the fifth above ground, that is, and almost the highest. Above that there was only the sixth floor, the Director-General's. The 'B' was consistent with all previous correspondence from my Director and was, I assumed, a code name, one which I had sometimes speculated might indicate considerable seniority within the Faculty's leadership, if the Director-General himself could be assumed to be 'A'. (I had never received any communication from the Director-General.) The memorandum invited or instructed me to report to Director B's office that afternoon, which was not merely unusual, but unprecedented, in my experience. I had never visited the fifth floor. I cannot, of course, speak for everyone. So I was not altogether surprised when the Executive Assistant who greeted me did not ask if I would like tea or coffee or offer me a seat in the waiting area while she checked that the Director was ready to see me, but instead told me that B was not there and directed me herself to a room nine or ten floors below, where, she said, the Director had asked to meet me.

This must have been at a time when I had been promoted to Divisional Director myself, or I would not have had an office of my own to be summoned from. It must therefore have been some time after Gibbon's disappearance, and after the case I took from Simmons that might or might not have been a crock of shit. The case was still technically open, but by then I had thought little – and done nothing – about it for many months, if not years.

The Assistant's directions were less than precise, and I

soon found myself unsure of my whereabouts. I had begun to suspect that, at one of the many intersections of indistinguishable corridors, I may have turned left when I should have turned right or – perhaps more likely – turned right when I should have gone right on, that is, straight on, and that, in one way or another, I was not where I was supposed to be, when I came across a door that, unlike all the other doors I had passed on that subterranean corridor, stood half open. Beyond it was an empty basement room. Empty of people, I should say, although it contained a table and three chairs, a bank of recording equipment and, on the left-hand wall (from where I was standing), a window – through which I could see a second, adjacent room. The walls of this second room were bare. At the back, unrolled on the concrete floor, was a thin, dirty mattress, on which lay a fat, heavily-creased paperback; in one corner, a galvanized iron bucket and an enamel bowl; and, in the centre of the room, a low, square table, perhaps eighteen inches high, in the form of a solid wooden block, almost a cube, but slightly less tall than it was wide, with stubby rounded feet, like a footstool, or a pouffe, I recall thinking, and simultaneously wondering if that was the word I was looking for, or might not be inappropriate for what was clearly an interrogation cell. The top of the block, or table, was decorated with straight black lines that formed a precise grid, on the intersections of which were placed a dozen polished, perfectly circular, doubly convex stones: six black, six white. Behind the table, facing the window (and therefore facing me) although not looking at either, looking in fact solely at the table, with a seventh black stone held delicately between the index and middle fingers of his left hand, while his right hand remained out of sight behind his back, knelt a man with a shaven head and a long, black, unkempt beard, wearing wire-rimmed glasses and an orange jumpsuit.

Looking back, I wonder about the possible confusion of turning right and going right on that may have taken me there. 'Right' can mean not only a direction (or two directions), but can also be an adjective with at least two meanings (being correct, or politically conservative) or a noun (referring to an entitlement, possibly inalienable). I recall Mary saying that these repetitions, elisions and contradictions are not confined to English: they occur also in German (*recht*), in French (*droit*) and in Spanish (*derecho*) and, for all she knew, in other languages with which she was less familiar. These confused and potentially confusing 'rights' are buried deep in the Enlightenment and are present at the heart of its most famous manifestos, she said. I can picture her now at our kitchen table, one Friday night after we had both returned from work, with two or three colleagues and couple of her friends from university, each with a glass of wine or a bottle of beer in our hand. I can see her, one eye closed against the smoke coiling up from the cigarette between her lips, saying they were present in its – the Enlightenment's – most ambitious statement of all; or rather, she corrected herself, in its greatest, least apologetic avowal of hope over experience: the Universal Declaration of Human Rights, the fifth article of which, as she, and I, and all our colleagues learned early in our careers at the Faculty, states that no one shall be subjected to torture or to cruel, inhuman or degrading treatment or punishment. An inch of ash fell from the end of her cigarette into the salad dressing smeared around her plate.

The man in the orange jumpsuit remained motionless

apart from a slight tremor in the fingers that held the stone. I had no idea how long he had been kneeling there contemplating his next move before I arrived but, as a matter of habit (already envisaging the report I would have to file of this encounter) I checked my watch when I first saw him and could say with some confidence that it was forty-seven minutes later that he finally placed his stone – randomly, as far as I could tell – well away from any of the others, some two or three points from the edge of an otherwise empty corner of the board. Throughout those forty-seven minutes, during which he had not once raised his eyes from the board, or looked up at the window – which, I guessed, would not have looked like a window from his point of view – I continued to watch, fascinated, at first losing my sense of time and then becoming more than usually aware of it, checking my watch at regular intervals, unable on each occasion to believe that the man in the next room would not place the stone in his hand on the board at the very next moment. The window through which I observed all this would look to him like a mirror, perhaps, or a blank computer screen, switched off and without power. He would not have been able to see me, even if he had looked.

Once he had finally placed the stone on the board he rocked back on his heels and rose into a crouch – an awkward, lop-sided stance – and I saw that his right hand was manacled to a ring bolt set into the floor in the centre of the room, that the chain was too short to allow him to stand upright, and that, beneath the jumpsuit, he was wearing flip-flops.

He straightened his legs and touched his toes, lifted his torso as far as the chain at his right wrist would allow, then sank to touch his toes again. After a while he lay face down on the bare floor and then slowly pushed himself up, his back and legs straight, the tip of his beard never quite clearing the floor before he sank down once, then up, then down – a dozen times, I counted, a slight pause; then two dozen – before returning to kneel behind the low table with the precise grid marked out on its surface, looking exactly as he had, and as it had, when I first found the basement room some fifty-five minutes earlier, except that now there were thirteen stones, six white, seven black. In this game it appeared that black went first, white followed. Later, once he had taught me the rules of Go – there are only two, he said, the second of which (the *rule of ko*) exists only to prevent the possibility of deadlock, of permanent stasis that arises from time to time from the operation of the first (the *rule of liberty*) – he would go on to explain that the possible combination of moves is virtually incalculable, or at least, when calculated, is incomprehensibly large. The number of positions in a single game, he said, is three (because each point on the grid can be either white, black or empty) to the power of three hundred and sixty-one (the number of points on a full-size, nineteen-by-nineteen grid) – or roughly ten to the power of one hundred and seventy-eight; that is, he said, ten times ten times ten, and so on, one hundred and seventy-eight times. But even that was nothing compared to the number of possible games, which was, he said, commonly held to be, three hundred and sixty-one bang.

"Bang?"

He drew an exclamation mark in the air and explained that, to a mathematician, it indicated not surprise but the product of all the integers comprising any given number. In this case, 361 times 360 times 359 times 358 . . . and so on down to one – or rather, in practice, he said, smiling, down to two, as multiplying by one of course makes no difference to the sum; where was he?

"Three sixty-one bang," I said.

"Right. Which is approximately ten to the power of seven hundred and eighty-two, a number I think you'll agree is not possible to conceive?"

I nodded. Beneath the prisoner's precise diction I thought I could still detect the faint trace of an American accent.

"But which," he said, "still isn't as large as the number of possible permutations according to other arguments, and other calculations I won't bore you with."

By the time he told me this, he had already beaten me two or three times using less than a quarter of the board: the smaller nine-by-nine grid on which beginners learn the rudiments of the game. Some time later he would tell me that the vast and unimaginable range of possibilities arose from the very simplicity of the game's premise. It was a common misconception, he would explain, possibly as a way of refraining from comment on whatever gauche and ill-advised move I had just made, that complexity arose from complexity, rather than from simplicity. It was precisely the simplicity of Go that made its outcomes so innumerable, while the complexity of, say, chess – with all its finicky rules governing the movement and capture of different pieces – in fact limited the potential number of moves in any given game, and therefore the total number of potential games. Despite all that, he would tell me, despite the, to all intents and purposes, boundless possibilities of Go, the advantage of being black, of playing first, is so great that, at least in games between players of comparable skill and expertise, it should lead to victory seven times out of ten.

"Which is always worth a bet," he said.

He compared the experience of playing Go to the age-old conflict between man's sense of free will – of the possibility of choice – and God's foreknowledge of our outcomes; of the battle, as some saw it, between the ritual of religion and the gift of grace. "Augustine would have understood," he said, nodding towards the fat paperback on his bedroll.

"Are you a gambling man?" he said.

He and I were not players of comparable skill, however, and once we started playing regularly it became clear that even with a handicap of four, five, six or even seven stones I would lose many more times than three in ten; I would have been lucky – I would have to have played exceptionally well – to win so much as once.

That first time I saw him, though, after he had finished his exercises and reviewed the board for several minutes, he leaned back, lifted his head and looked at the window, apparently at me. I did not recognize him then, it being some years since I had looked at the photographs in the reports from Operations and Interrogations, and many months since I had last, fleetingly, thought about him or his whereabouts – which, had I considered the matter, I would probably have assumed to be a cell not unlike this one, perhaps, but certainly not *this one* – which I had not known existed – and not here, in the Faculty, a matter of yards, of half a dozen flights of stairs from my own office, but rather somewhere far away, in another country, in all likelihood, another continent. I knew he could not see me through the window and could not know that I was there, given that my presence was accidental and, surely, unauthorized, the result of a mistake on my part, a confusion between turning right and carrying right on. Nevertheless, he looked into the room he could not see, into the eyes of a man he could not know was there, and said:

"White to play."

The *rule of liberty* states that every stone remaining on the board must have at least one open "point" (an intersection, called a "liberty") directly adjacent to it (up, down, left or right), or must be part of a group of stones of the same colour that has at least one such "liberty" adjacent to it. Stones (or groups of stones) that lose their last liberty are captured and removed from the board. Stones or groups of stones that cannot avoid having all their remaining liberties occupied by the opposing player's stones – even though the opponent has not yet placed them, and is, perhaps, biding his or her time, conducting more urgent business elsewhere on the board, where the outcome is less certain – such stones are "dead"; those secure in their territory, or where the outcome is as yet uncertain, except perhaps to God or to the most skilful players able to calculate a dozen or more moves into the future, are said to be "alive".

"How was your day?"

That again?

It isn't supposed to be like this. Stephen grew up and left home. He went to university, took his degree. He is a philosopher, just like his mother. But here he is, back in the family home that hasn't been a family home for almost twenty years, asking me about my day as if nothing has happened. Nothing has happened, of course, but still: this is not the way it is supposed to be. In a better-ordered universe, Stephen wouldn't be here, now, cooking dinner.

In that universe Stephen would pretty much ignore me for two or three decades and build a life of his own. Eventually, awareness of his own advancing age would lead him prematurely to recognize the proximity of my death, and he would re-establish relations. A couple more decades would follow, during which my death, whilst approaching ever closer, would nonetheless seem to him as if it were never actually going to happen, a couple of decades in which his re-established visits would become increasingly formulaic until, eventually, I would experience some debilitating physical deterioration – a stroke perhaps, or dementia – that would fundamentally change the nature of our relationship until, finally, I would die, and Stephen would be relieved of the obligation he had inherited at birth along with the guilt of having been born at all.

That, broadly, is how his life should go.

Perhaps there is still time?

But here he is, largely unchanged. He has more books, stacked in precarious ziggurats around his room, piled beside the cello case that has stood, untouched, since he left home. He has aged, but not by much. The acne has gone, the shadow around his jaw is more defined, his forehead more pronounced, his hairline receding at the temples. He is only twenty-two, and it seems a little like bad luck, but is of course not luck at all, merely inheritance.

He moved back on Saturday, slept for most of Sunday and was still in bed this morning when I left for work.

"What are you doing now?" he asks.

"If I told you that . . ."

"You'd have to kill me. I know, Dad. But is it still the same?"

"Pretty much."

Is it, though?

The plots and bombs and guns and raids and reports are all the same, of course – when you get down to it, there are only so many permutations available to the perpetrators of atrocity. But has my own role changed? Was I a Divisional Director when he left? Did I have an office of my own on the fourth floor and the responsibility of managing the team I'd previously been a part of?

I'm fairly sure Gibbon had disappeared some time before Stephen left home – a year before? More? We didn't see much of him, even before he disappeared; and, for some time afterwards, there seemed to be no let up in the flow of memoranda.

Had I moved into his office before Stephen left home? Had I been promoted into Gibbon's job – or at least assumed his duties?

Probably I had.

Had I discovered the floors below the Crypt at that time, though?

Had I met the Director-General, then?

Probably not.

Does it matter? When Stephen asks what I'm up to these days, he's not looking for a detailed comparison between my job descriptions now and when he left.

He is asking something else entirely.

I say, "How's Emma?"

I've never met Emma, but I know Stephen spent Christmas somewhere in the southern hemisphere with her family. He sent a postcard from the airport at Cape Town. He has never described her as his girlfriend – or in any other way that might give me some clue about the nature of their relationship – but I assume she is of some importance to him.

"We're talking about you, Dad."

Are we? Aren't we just making conversation?

"There's not much to say about me."

SOME YEARS AGO – while I was still working on the third floor, sharing an open office with Simmons and Leach and Butler – I received a memorandum very similar to the one I received on the morning I am not now describing to Stephen, the morning I played my first move at Go. That memorandum – the earlier memorandum – had also been signed 'B': it invited me to report to the fourth floor, to Gibbon's office. In all the years I'd worked at the Faculty, I had only ever been there twice and on neither occasion had it, strictly speaking, been Gibbon's office. The most recent had been the night there were no bombs in the railway stations, and no trains, when we had slept in the office and I had woken early and explored what was by then already no longer Gibbon's office, Gibbon having disappeared, and had found the tube of moisturiser identical to the tube Butler had given me, the night I'd seen the painting of the princess and her servants, the painter, the courtiers and, quite possibly, the king and queen of Spain, all staring at me, or rather, at the point where I was sitting, just behind Gibbon's desk. That picture had replaced the framed print of a fox hunt I remembered from the first and only other time I'd been there, shortly after Mary's death, when Gibbon's predecessor felt an unprecedented need – or, more likely, had been strongly advised – to speak to me man-to-man, as it were, to express the Faculty's sympathy, to ask how I was getting on and say that if there were anything he, or the Faculty, could do – anything, that is, beyond the bereavement counselling I had already been offered, and refused, and had subsequently received written instruction, from Gibbon's predecessor himself, to attend – then I should only ask. His door was always open, he said, glancing involuntarily over my shoulder at the door, which was closed. At least figuratively, he added; obviously he couldn't really keep it open, that would be absurd, and quite possibly a breach of security. I had nodded and thanked him, but said that I was fine. Really, I was fine.

The third time, then, that I approached Gibbon's office, I was greeted by his Executive Assistant: a short, dark-haired woman with what I thought might be a trace of a Welsh accent, but might not, and who, I would shortly discover, was no longer Gibbon's Executive Assistant, and was called Bernadette. She did not offer a surname. She welcomed me and showed me directly into the empty office, and stood, waiting, by the door. It was furnished with the same desk, chairs and filing cabinets that had been there on my two previous visits; the same heavy net curtains, through which a little sunshine leaked, still covered the small, north-facing window; and on the opposite wall the huge picture of the Spanish court still gazed with a dozen pairs of eyes malevolently down at a point just behind the desk. On the desk itself, on a dark green blotter between the in-tray and the out-tray – both of which were empty – lay a plain white envelope, addressed to me. I approached the desk and, without yet sitting down, opened the envelope to find a brief, typewritten note welcoming me to my new office and telling me that, if I needed anything, I should just ask. It was signed 'B'. Unlike the memorandum, the B was handwritten, in blue ink, with a certain confident flourish. "Is there anything I can get you, sir?" Bernadette said from behind me. I asked her, please, to call me Mr Exley.

On the fifteenth day of the following month I discovered that my salary had increased. In the weeks that followed I began to receive written instructions from B, much as I had previously from Gibbon, even after he seemed to have disappeared. When I wrote back, on any subject beyond routine progress reports – which I amalgamated from the reports of Simmons, Leach and Butler, and subsequently Hargreaves – B's responses appeared friendly, or at least polite. When I summoned the courage to ask about removing or replacing the Spanish print – which I knew by then to be a reproduction of Velazquez's *Las Meninas*, a fact which made its unsettling gaze no less oppressive – B advised me to ask Bernadette for the catalogue. I discovered that all of the artwork in the Faculty's offices was borrowed from the Government's extensive collection: I could select any picture I wished from the category suitable to my level of seniority. As there were no original works available below Director grade, I chose a limited-edition print of Patrick Caulfield's *Still Life with Dagger*, which was all surface and outline and had no depth whatsoever. After the Velazquez, it was a relief.

A month or so after I moved into what was now undoubtedly my office, B also suggested that I might consider changing my allegiance from the Butcher's Arms – which, despite the increase in my disposable income, I had not visited since my promotion – to the Lamb & Flag, where I might meet my fellow Divisional Directors. There were five of us, it turned out (there may have been others who did not come to the pub, as Butler had not, and presumably still did not), each responsible, I assumed – we did not discuss work, obviously – for a team of four or five investigators, each of whom would be commissioning Operations to observe, infiltrate and disrupt the activities of countless persons of interest, commissioning Interrogation teams to extract what intelligence they could from those detained, assessing the results, making connections and reporting to their Divisional Directors, who, like me, would assess, evaluate, make further connections and report to B, who would respond, in my experience at least, with encouragement and a generalized, unspecific praise that, while welcome, added nothing to our understanding of the progress of our crusade against terror. Later, as I watched the man in the orange jumpsuit appear to watch me, and to await some response, apparently from me – even though he could neither see me nor know that I was there – I doubted that B would be so congenial.

It had been almost an hour since I must have misunderstood my directions and discovered the interrogation and observation rooms that I should not have discovered. Having spent so long watching the man in the orange jumpsuit play a single move in his game against an opponent who was not there to observe it, I had to assume that I had not only missed my way, but also my appointment. I was doubly, or triply, at fault: in a room I had no right to be in, observing a man I had no right to see, having left B somewhere, I had to assume, not far away, but not where I was, twiddling his thumbs (if he were a man) or her thumbs (if she were not) and wondering where on earth I'd got to. Wondering too, in all likelihood, why I couldn't follow a simple instruction, and beginning to doubt, given that I obviously couldn't be trusted to find my way around a building I had worked in for more than twenty years, whether I should be trusted with more important matters, such as the detection, assessment and disruption of plans to terrorize millions of my fellow citizens.

I was an hour late for our meeting and there was no explanation I could give that would not make me appear both incompetent and untrustworthy. The prisoner's words, however – "White to play" – indicated that he expected someone – White – to appear, and at least a strong possibility that his expectation would be met, given the evidence that White had made six previous moves. As he had addressed his invitation to the window, or screen, it also seemed reasonable to suppose that when White did appear, he or she would do so here, in the observation room, and not next door in the interrogation room. At which point I would be discovered and invited to explain myself, which I couldn't. My anxiety was only reinforced when the man in the orange jumpsuit picked a white stone from a bowl in front of the table and held it aloft between the index and middle finger of his left hand while waiting for a response. Alternatively, if White did not appear, the prisoner might become impatient, or angry, or distressed and seek to raise the alarm or somehow attract the attention of the security guards who must, I knew, be somewhere in the vicinity, although I had seen no one but the prisoner himself in the hour I'd now spent below ground level. If the guards came I would also be discovered and called upon to explain myself, which would be difficult. I had to forestall that possibility. I looked at the board, at the last black stone to be played. I said, "Go next to your last move."

The prisoner appeared to hear nothing. I turned to the desk, with its array of recording equipment. Somewhere there would be a switch that allowed communication with the interrogation room. I was not an interrogator myself, but over the years I had read many reports and transcripts of the process, and had attended some of the training and legal briefings arranged for the interrogators. I knew that, while the room I stood in was primarily for observation and recording, it would also sometimes be appropriate, as one of the tools available to the interrogation team, one of the tricks of the trade, so to speak, for an unobserved, invisible observer to address the interrogator, or even to address the prisoner directly, in order to guide interrogations, to express encouragement or disbelief or derision at what was being said, to imitate the voice of God, to seal a deal that was being offered and accepted, or to seem to do so in the interests of coaxing or intimidating or simply disorientating the prisoner. When I found the switch and flicked it, I said again: "White plays next to your last move." The man in the jumpsuit seemed confused, and gestured help-lessly toward the board. There were, of course, four points immediately adjacent to the last black stone he had played – up, down, left and right – all empty, plus four more diagonally adjacent points that might also, loosely, have been described as next to it. I realized that my broad, unhelpful instruction had left him with eight possible alternative interpretations of my intention. I was not an interrogator but from what I knew of the process it was likely that a prisoner who had been subjected to extensive and prolonged interrogation – which it seemed likely this man had – would be highly sensitive to ambiguous instructions in which the correct, desired action or response was not immediately obvious. Such a prisoner might, in the face of such ambiguity, rapidly demonstrate a significant increase in stress, with a corresponding likeli-hood of impaired rationality and/or enhanced compliance as uncertainty multiplied the fear of saying or doing the wrong thing, the thing that was not desired or expected, and of the consequences that might follow; such ambiguity was, indeed, another of the interrogator's tricks of the trade.

I had never played this game, but as a child I had played another on a similar grid, where the squares, rather than the points, represented the sea and the object was to guess the location of your opponent's ships, and sink them. I quickly counted up from the bottom and in from the side of the board and said, "D-17". The man relaxed, the tension draining from his neck and shoulders, from the way he held his head. He sat back on his heels and placed the white stone on the board diagonally adjacent to his own last play. He picked a black stone from a pot I could not see behind the table and began to contemplate the board again.

I had miscounted: the play he made on my behalf was not the play I had intended. I'd meant D-16, directly to the right, as I looked at it, of the black stone. However, I thought it unwise, and possibly unfair, or inadmissible within the rules of a game I did not yet know, at this stage to amend or correct my move. Besides, I had no idea what I was doing, no idea whether the move I had in fact made, or had mis-instructed the prisoner to make on my behalf, was any better or worse than the one I had intended.

His reaction gave me the impression it was at least not the move he had been expecting, which I regarded as a good sign. He stared at the board, turning his head from side to side, squinting at my stone from the corner of one eye and then the corner of the other, like a blackbird sizing up a worm that might turn out to be a rubber band. He exhaled two or three times briefly, fiercely. He dropped his black stone back in to the pot, then drew out a handful more and allowed them to trickle through his fingers with a sound like a faint waterfall. He looked up at the window, at the screen, with a quizzical air, as if at a parrot which had not only spoken, but had said something unexpectedly apropos.

I could tell Stephen all that, but I don't.

THE TRUTH IS that when Stephen asks how my day has been, again, today, after coming home on Saturday and spending all of yesterday in bed, this particular Monday has been only superficially identical to all my previous working days: a crowded, sweaty train; a morning spent reviewing and allocating new cases, summarizing reports for onward transmission to B; an afternoon talking to the prisoner in the orange jumpsuit and playing Go in the interrogation room several floors below ground level; a drink after work, a less crowded train home. But there is a difference.

I have been visiting the prisoner every afternoon, or almost every afternoon, for several years now. I have learned to play Go and today, for the first time since I fully appreciated just how difficult it was going to be, I have glimpsed the possibility of winning.

At the end of our session, as tradition dictates, I left my last play not on the board, but marked on a paper grid, folded and secured within a sealed envelope. I signed the envelope across the seal and he counter-signed it. Tomorrow he will break open the envelope and see what I have done.

I am looking forward to tomorrow.

I don't say this, however, not even to myself. I don't tell Stephen about the prisoner, or about Go. I ask him what he's going to do next.

"Dad? I only just got home."

I don't say that it isn't his home now, that he has left.

"You must have some idea?"

He shakes his head, more in disillusion than disagreement. He is disappointed in me.

He says, "I could always join the Faculty."

When I say nothing he says he's only joking.

# TWO

I DO NOT tell Stephen about the prisoner in the orange jumpsuit and flip-flops, or about the basement room somewhere below the Crypt, or what happened after I made that first move, my first move as White, because, obviously, if I do, I will have to kill him.

There are other options available to me, other things I could tell him, things that are not about work, are not secret, or at least not secret in that sense. I could, for example, tell him about the diagnosis. I'm fairly sure that happened after he left home. It is certainly not something we have ever discussed.

It may have started before he left. In fact, I think it did. The itching certainly began long ago, years ago, before Stephen was even born. It was mostly on my legs then, my hands, in patches of dry skin; it was only later that it seemed to concentrate itself around my anus. The itching was not, in the end, related to the diagnosis – not the diagnosis that matters – but it did, indirectly, lead me to it. I recall – even now, four or five years later – the conversation with the pharmacist, recall the bathos of the word "haemorrhoids", and the kick of energy contained in the phrase "colorectal cancer".

The ointment helped, although I resented the preposterous precision required not to leave brown shit marks on the towel when I washed and dried my arse before applying the slippery clear gel each morning and evening. I resented, too, the initial sting as it came into contact with the tiny scratches

I had made to the delicate, swollen perianal skin; resented, frankly, having to acknowledge, to touch and push back inside myself, back into my rectum, the beads of flesh that slipped out with my stools but which were still, in some way, part of me. Nonetheless, under the influence of the ointment, and perhaps of my more than usually careful hygiene, the itching reduced. I had to give it that. The soreness faded and cleared up altogether, and then returned; now it fades, and returns in a causeless, unfathomable cycle that will end only with my death, but which is, perhaps, the least of my worries.

It was on my fourth or fifth visit to the pharmacy to re-plenish supplies – by which time, I am as certain as I can be, Stephen had left home for university – that the pharmacist asked if I was sure there had been no blood in my stool, and I admitted that, yes, there had. That it had been there, on and off, since the second or third tube of ointment. The pharma-cist insisted that I visit a doctor.

"But the ointment works," I said.

I had piles. Hadn't I touched them? Hadn't I eased them back into the safe, dark cavern of my bowels?

"All the same," the pharmacist said.

The possibility that this might not be a case of either/or but *both* hovered above the counter between us. As she held out the white paper bag with a green cross printed on it, she said: "Go to see your doctor. Please."

I reached out to take the bag, but she would not relinquish it until I said, "I will."

I supposed this was her job; in my mind, I forgave her.

It took a month, maybe more. A month in which, if I remember correctly, a crude, homemade nail bomb – or a nail bomb expertly constructed to appear crude and homemade:

we had learned to be careful in the inferences we drew – exploded in a crowded supermarket, killing sixteen and injuring dozens more; a month in which a man entering a football stadium was detained while carrying a canister of sarin; a month in which a cache of C4 plastic explosive – a cache wholly unrelated, as far as we were aware, to the case I'd taken on from Simmons, the crock of shit, which by that time had I think already entered the quiet phase, the phase before I myself met Volorik and became more directly involved. If it was not that month, it was another much like it, before I telephoned the doctor's surgery and spoke to a bored, incurious receptionist and made an appointment for the end of the following week. I asked myself why I had delayed making the appointment for so long.

Why the delay?

It was not pressure of work, I knew, merely the desire to maintain a state of uncertainty, to prevent the possibility of cancer or not-cancer from collapsing into the certainty that there might, after all, be nothing seriously wrong with me, and that I might, in fact, have to go on like this.

Hope was an unaccustomed emotion, then, and slippery with it.

I booked a day's leave and told Bernadette – who had no reason and probably no desire to know – that my son, Stephen, was coming home from university for a long weekend, an unnecessary lie that I immediately regretted. Now I would have to invent three day's worth of father-son activity in case she asked how my weekend had been.

Eventually, on a Friday morning, I found myself sitting in the surgery waiting area, shifting my buttocks uncomfortably on the vinyl covered bench – the itching had returned with a vengeance; and with it the sharp, stabbing pain – while I flipped through leaflets on type-2 diabetes and sexually transmitted disease. I rolled one into a straw, blew gently through it and flattened it out again. It was not so much death that I was hoping for, I thought, but the death sentence. A period of grace in which death was inevitable and I could no longer be expected to *do anything*. But was not death, by definition, always inevitable, sooner or later? What difference, really, would a diagnosis make?

I was almost disappointed when the receptionist called my name.

I had only met the doctor once before on my own account, when my neck had inexplicably locked in an excruciating spasm: he had prescribed a combination of clinical-grade painkillers and anti-depressants that agreeably obliterated the following three days. I had met him countless times, however, as a father, as Stephen progressed through the usual gamut of childhood illnesses. I always thought him avuncular, but it was a second-hand idea, a weightless simile: I had no uncle, no older relative at all, much less one who combined a broad stomach, a twinkling sea-green eye and limitless access to prescription narcotics.

"We'd better take a look," he said, when I explained the reason for my visit.

"What are you looking for?"

"Well, up past the haemorrhoids we might just find us some bowel polyps."

Polyp is a beautiful word, I thought. I had a brief aquatic vision of delicate translucent jellyfish pulsing through warm tropical water, backlit for the camera, and of purple anemones, stubbornly in-folded at low tide.

"Are polyps bad?"

"They're not good. To be fair, they're common as muck and mostly harmless. But once in a while the little beggars grow up to be tumours. So we scrape them all off, just to be sure."

He smiled as if he had just explained the necessity of weeding a flowerbed, or sanding down a window frame before re-painting it. He looked like the kind of man who might relax with a little gardening or DIY. Avuncular, if you had that kind of uncle.

But the word "scrape" lodged in my mind. The man was going to *scrape* out my backside?

"The colonoscope has a wire, a bit like a cheese wire, with an electric current running through it. We loop it round the polyp and . . . snip!"

I felt sick. Of course, I probably was sick, but this was different. I'd been irritated – physically, by the discomfort of my anus, and mentally, by the disruption of my routine and equilibrium – but I hadn't been ill. I had been looking forward to observing my own possible reaction to being told that I had bowel cancer. I had envisaged hours of quiet fortitude, of working out what I would do with the weeks, or months, or years that might remain to me (nothing). Who would I tell? (No one; or not until it was far too late.) What would I prioritize at work? (Nothing.) What books would I read? (What did it matter?) But now, when it came to it, I just felt queasy. The man was going to scrape me out like a blocked drain. Whether I had cancer or not.

I said, "You are joking?"

He was smiling, after all.

"I'm not, Mr Exley. It's a perfectly standard procedure."

He swung round in his chair to face the cabinet behind

him, and began rattling through a deep drawer full of glass and steel contraptions, the purpose of which I could only guess, but preferred not to.

"Now?"

The doctor stood up, motioned for me to do the same.

"Now seems like as good a time as any."

WHEN I FIRST met Mary she talked a lot about St Augustine.

When we say, "When I first did this-or-that" or "first met so-and-so", we don't mean it. We mean something less defined: "in the early days of the activity or relationship". Or: "before I knew better". But Mary really had talked about St Augustine the first time we met, in the wine bar to which a colleague had invited us both for a reason.

My role at the Faculty was different then.

The bar was bigger than it looked from the entrance under a railway bridge, but many of the tables occupied their own niches beneath brick arches, and it was easy to be left to oneself.

Mary said she'd been studying Philosophy and I asked her what she thought she might do next. I knew what she had studied, and where. I'd read a précis of her doctoral thesis. Despite appearances, this was not a blind date.

She shrugged. She told me Augustine had a theory of the relativity of time that Einstein might have recognized. For humans, she said, time has three tenses: past, present, future.

I nodded.

It was not like that for God, she said, for whom there was no difference between the three. God's knowledge does not change, which was just another way of saying that, for God, there is no time.

"So far, so simple," she said.

I agreed.

"But it's not really that simple. Because the three tenses only exist in the human mind, which itself exists only in the present. The past is just the recollection of a present human mind; the future exists only as anticipation in the present."

"So the time is always now?"

My colleague, a woman who had been at school with Mary, subsequently lost touch, but recently bumped into her not once but twice in the local park – what were the odds? – said now was the time to buy another bottle. She sat back, trying to catch the attention of a waiter.

"Now is always a good time," Mary said.

I said, "But only for God?"

"For all of us."

By "good" she meant appropriate. Did she already know what it was that we were talking about?

She raised her glass to her lips without taking her eyes off mine.

Having ordered, my colleague blundered back into the conversation. "The mind that remembers and anticipates? How do we know it exists?"

I said, "Descartes? *Cogito ergo sum?*"

Like most people who know nothing about philosophy, I knew that.

Mary smiled. "Augustine got there first, again. *For just as I know that I exist, I know that I know.*"

"But what if you're wrong?"

"*If I am mistaken, I exist,*" she said, emptying her wineglass. "That's Augustine, too, by the way. Not me."

"And you?"

"I don't think it matters."

"But you're the philosopher."

"What I mean is, we have nothing to lose. If we behave *as if* we exist, *as if* time exists and there's a future that will be different from the present, what difference would it make if we were wrong?"

I felt a sudden familiar weariness seep through me. "It would all have been a monumental waste of effort?"

"So what? If you don't exist, what have you wasted?"

The second bottle arrived, and fresh glasses. It was that kind of place. We stopped talking while the waiter offered my colleague the chance to taste the wine. When he left, Mary said, "If you exist you're going to die. If you exist there will be a future that is different, if only in that you won't be in it."

"Which might be a good thing."

"It might. It might not. It all depends what other differences you make."

"Does it matter?"

"Why not behave as if it did?"

Which, on reflection, I'm not sure she believed, or believed all the time, but was where I pulled the conversation back to her future, to what she might do to make a difference, what – the words stuck in my craw, every time – she might do for her country.

# I KNEW I SHOULD HAVE LEFT

T HE MAN IN the orange jumpsuit gradually settled, stopped moving his head from side to side, stopped grabbing fistfuls of stones and letting them trickle back into the pot I could not see. He closed his eyes and breathed deeply. After a minute or two, he re-opened his eyes, took a single black stone between the index and middle fingers of his left hand and began to study the board again.

I knew I should have left. I should have returned above ground, to my office on the fourth floor; or to the fifth, perhaps, to ask B's Executive Assistant to clarify her directions and to apologize to B on my behalf if, as seemed likely, it was already too late to resume my appointment. I knew the longer I remained, the more I would compound my error, the more I would increase the risk of being discovered somewhere I should not have been, with a prisoner I should not have known about, in an interrogation suite I should not have known existed. I knew all that. But still I found I could not leave.

I was spellbound by the sight of the prisoner's hand hovering over the board while, expressionless and without any movement other than the slight trembling in his outstretched fingers, he calculated his next move. I could not leave before that move was made. It was not that I was curious to see what it would be – I was not yet familiar with the game, and his next move was likely to be as unintelligible to me, as apparently random, as his last, or as my own – but I *was* curious to see how long it might take for him to make it. With the board largely empty, there were countless choices available; to me it seemed that sheer abundance made the choice not so much difficult as redundant. With so many possibilities it would be incomprehensibly difficult to calculate the impact of any individual move; more to the point, it would be meaningless. Surely nothing that happened now, at this stage of the game, when there remained vast tracts of unoccupied territory to fill, could make that much difference to the outcome? But the minutes ticked by: ten, fifteen, twenty. Was anything, I wondered, worth contemplating so hard for so long?

At that point, his lecture on probability and Go's complexity lay sometime in our future.

Just as he seemed to have decided where to place the next black stone, just as his hand lowered towards the board, we were both – he and I – startled by a voice from behind me.

"Your move was unorthodox. I can see why he had to recalculate."

It was a woman's voice. I turned to find Butler standing in the doorway of the observation room.

WHEN STEPHEN ASKS me what I'm doing now, and I don't tell him about the man in the orange jumpsuit, or about the cancer diagnosis, either, and he won't tell me about Emma or what, if anything, he's planning to do now, I think we might run out of things to say. There is a pause, a silence, which he eventually ends by saying: "You never ask about my day."

Which I know is a joke.

Since he returned, he's spent one day in bed and another – today – doing what? Sitting on the sofa – which I tell myself is no longer *the* sofa, after all: it is *my* sofa, even if it is exactly the same sofa it had always been. The point is that he no longer lives here, not what he does while I'm at work. And yet, here he is, standing by the stove, cooking dinner like he always used to, wearing an apron I don't recognize and possibly isn't even mine.

He says, "I did a bit of spring cleaning."

I thank him, and he says: "When did you last clean out the kitchen cupboards?"

The truth, of course – he knows this and is only asking for effect – is that I have never cleaned out the cupboards. Not the ones he means, with all the plates and glasses and coffee cups and flower vases I don't use and the appliances I haven't taken out of their boxes since the last time he was here; somewhere in there, if I remember rightly, is a gravy boat with scalloped edges and gold leaf decorations that Mary's grandparents gave us when we married. It's not that I avoid cleaning cupboards: it's just not something that ever occurs to me. I can't recall anyone – not even Stephen, when he lived here – ever doing so. Mary certainly never did anything of the sort. She was far too busy working, having Stephen, and working more. The bright future, the rapid promotion and increasing responsibility that our superiors planned for her could not be dimmed, and was not dimmed, by a swerve into motherhood. They had their reservations, of course, which they almost suppressed in her presence, but which made her all the more determined to prove them wrong. When she became pregnant for the second time, it also became clear that she was trying their patience. Having procreated once might be unfortunate, they hinted, but what did twice look like? Not as much like carelessness, it turns out, as stepping into the road outside the hospital. Until that moment she had worked, we had both worked; we'd looked after Stephen and washed our clothes and even ironed a few; we'd cooked and scrubbed the dishes and cleaned, insofar as we had cleaned at all, without either one of us ever feeling the need to clean out the kitchen cupboards.

Perhaps I had not been paying sufficient attention.

I say, "Isn't that what silver fish are for?"

He doesn't laugh. He has no idea what silver fish might be.

More neutrally, I say, "Were they dirty?"

"Filthy. And the glasses were all over the place."

The glasses had been in the cupboard. It's where they live.

I don't think my mother cleaned kitchen cupboards, either. If my father ever did it would have been at his beacon keeper's hut, where – according to Stephen's journal, at least – there was only one cupboard. If he cleaned at all, it would only have been to prove some point to Jacobs – just as Stephen is trying to prove some point to me. To test his patience, perhaps, or his sanity.

"Don't you remember, Dad, how you used to drive me nuts?"

I can't say that I do, or not in any way specifically related to cupboards.

"Whenever you put the glasses away, you stuck them any old where. Don't you remember?"

I put them in the cupboard. What else was I supposed to do?

"I would line them up," Stephen says. "All the tumblers together, the wine glasses together, in straight rows, in their place. That way you get more in and don't break anything. And you know where everything is when you want it."

I always know where the glasses are. They're in the cupboard.

"I never knew it bothered you."

He looks as if I've just confessed to a taste for eating babies: a mixture of horror and disbelief I don't know if I'm meant to take seriously.

"Really?"

He turns back to the stove. A thick tomato sauce has begun to bubble and spit.

"You never mentioned it."

He stirs the sauce, lights the burner underneath a second, larger pan of water. Not turning back, he says quietly, "She was the same."

"Who?"

I think he might mean Mary, though I can't see how he'd know.

He speaks so softly, and towards the cooker, that I can barely hear him.

"Emma."

"You split up with your girlfriend over how she put the glasses away?"

It probably isn't the most helpful thing to say.

He says, "I'm putting the spaghetti on. If you're going to change, you'd better do it now."

# WHAT PHILOSOPHERS ARE FOR

T HE PRISONER THREW the black stone at the screen. It bounced off with a soft click and landed somewhere I couldn't see. Butler stepped across to the desk and flicked the intercom switch, cutting off the sound of our voices, while we could hear him say: "What's going on?"

It was a reasonable question.

"Hello, Robert," Butler said. "Good to see you again."

Robert? For a moment I thought she must have been talking to someone else. The man in the next room, perhaps.

"Butler. What are you doing here?"

In the next room the prisoner rose to a crouch, turned away from us, away from the screen, and scooted as far back as the chain on his right wrist would allow. He bent and tugged the mattress towards him, then lay down, opened the fat paperback apparently at random, and made a show of trying to read. Or perhaps he was reading, but I didn't think so. He held up the book – ostentatiously, I thought – turning a page he'd obviously read a hundred times before, and I recognized the cover. I'd last seen it on Stephen's desk, next to his typewriter; but I had seen it frequently before that, long before that, in Mary's hands: St Augustine's *City of God*. Mary wrote her thesis about it, quoted from it the very first time we met, but she understood I might not want to read all eleven hundred pages for myself.

"That's what philosophers are for," she said. "We read these books so you don't have to."

"I knew there had to be something."

Butler smiled at me. The smile seemed genuine enough, suggesting affection rather than amusement, or perhaps a little of both.

"Why am I here? The same as you."

"Meeting your Director?"

This time amusement won. "I'm well acquainted with your Director," she said. "I'm here to learn Go."

Some of this made sense, but not much – not much of it, and not much sense. Butler knew my Director because she *was* my Director. She was "B", which, standing there in the observation room, I realized was obvious, and had not been code at all. Butler had sent the memo inviting me up to Gibbon's office, to what became my office; Butler had written the note to welcome me – had promoted me – into Gibbon's job. But Butler also reported to me. I allocated cases to her and she dealt with them and sent me her reports. She was in the team I managed, along with Simmons and Leach and Hargreaves, the new man I'd been assigned after I moved upstairs; she had a desk, still, on the third floor, that she left at five o'clock most days, carrying her fold-up bicycle into the lift.

It was a form of cover, I supposed, but a peculiar one. Were all the Directors masquerading as their own employees? Was Simmons actually the D-G? Or, worse still, Leach?

No. It couldn't be Leach. But Simmons?

What made no sense at all, even accepting that Butler was both my junior and my Director, was that she had arranged to meet me there, in the interrogation suite I was not supposed to know existed. That she had arranged for me to discover it, and to discover a man in an orange jumpsuit shackled to the floor.

"I want you to come here every day," she said. "Come about this time, if possible, and talk to him. I want you to learn Go."

"Why?"

I was looking into Butler's eyes, something I never did. I still couldn't say what colour they were.

She held my gaze. "I think you might find it instructive."

"I'm not an interrogator."

"And this will not be an interrogation."

"So what would I be doing?"

She turned away from me at last, turned back to the window into the next room, the interrogation cell, where the prisoner was lying on his thin dirty mattress reading *City of God* with apparent interest.

Butler said, "We'll see."

## THE SAME AS IN NEVER THE SAME

I HANG MY suit jacket in the wardrobe, and sit on the bed to untie my shoes. I can hear him downstairs, humming a cello suite he used to play, hear the dull clatter of a heavy frying pan on the top of the stove, and the soft, glottal chug of olive oil. I shut the bedroom door.

When I return to the kitchen, Stephen is setting the table, laying out forks and spoons and glasses – wineglasses – for us both. I open a bottle of wine.

He says, "They haven't stopped, then?"

"Who? Stopped what?"

"Next door. Knocking on the wall."

This again?

"They're different people."

The couple next door, on the side he always said the noise came from, moved in shortly after Mary and I, and stayed all the time Stephen was growing up. We had drinks a couple of times. He did something for a bank we never quite understood; she was an opera singer, she said, although she worked for an estate agent. We would hear her practising arpeggios, keeping her throat in shape. When Mary was pregnant the second time they said they were hoping to have children, too. It was why they'd bought the house. They never did, though; I don't know why. When Mary died the woman told me how sorry they both were, but we didn't talk much after that. They finally moved out a couple of years ago. The new owners don't look much older than Stephen. They already have children.

"It sounds the same."

I don't know what to say.

"The same as in never the same," he says. "No rhythm; no pattern."

"When did you hear it?"

He gives me the baby-eating look again.

"Just now, Dad. Five minutes ago. While you were changing."

I say nothing for a while. Then I say the meatballs smell good. I pour the wine.

While we eat, Stephen says, "Do you remember X?"

For a moment I wonder what he's talking about.

"I wrote about her. In my journal."

He does not say he wrote the journal in code and never showed it to me. I do not mention that I nonetheless took away each instalment to be decrypted. We do not need to discuss this.

I say, "Was she the one you were going to be in a play with?"

"The *Oresteia*."

"If you say so. What happened?"

"The same as Emma."

I can't stop myself. "She put the glasses in the wrong cupboard?"

"Something like that."

After dinner, Stephen goes up to his room, his old room, while I do the washing up. After a few minutes I hear the soft, arrhythmic pecking of a typewriter, his typewriter, Mary's old typewriter, that I gave him years ago.

I put away the clean crockery and turn on the news.

# THREE

WHEN THE DOCTOR'S receptionist called, inviting me to make an appointment, she insisted I come into the surgery. It was not something that could be dealt with by letter, or on the telephone, she said. At which point we'd effectively dealt with it already, because now I knew what the doctor would say. So I made an appointment, because it was easier that way, but didn't go, and didn't make another when she rang again, that afternoon. I asked her to stop ringing. I said my employers did not appreciate personal calls at the office. I explained I had no mobile phone and gave her my home number, which I never answered, anyway, except when Stephen's name came up on the screen, and not always, even then.

I didn't mention the cancer at work. There might come a time, I supposed, when it would no longer be possible to hide what was going on. If I lost weight, for example, in a way that couldn't be explained by some fictitious change in diet or life-style - some sudden interest in marathon running, or squash, or long-distance cycle-racing, say - or if the pain became something I could not disguise. I was hazy on the details, but by then I imagined it would already be too late. There would be nothing the Faculty could do. If I'd said anything to my superiors then, when I did not need to see the doctor to know what he would say, they would have felt obliged to respond. Not only personally - that is, awkwardly, as one human being to another – but bureaucratically, in order to protect the position of the Faculty itself.

When Mary died there had been no avoiding it; HR suggested counselling. When I declined, they insisted – or advised Gibbon's predecessor to insist. In Mary, the Faculty had lost one employee to arbitrary, ridiculous fate – one of its brightest rising stars, at that. Gibbon's predecessor did not say so, but I guessed they had no wish to lose another (even one less bright with no career to speak of) to spectacular grief, or to a deterioration of judgment arising from unspectacular but still debilitating depression. They would want to avoid the risk of collateral damage to operations, to morale and to the Faculty's reputation and legal standing in the event of that second employee's – that is, my – failure to cope.

The possibility that Mary's death might not affect my performance at all was not considered. It was only human to be incapacitated by the loss of those closest to us. And who would know that better than Human Resources? Not to be so incapacitated – at least not without intensive therapeutic intervention – might itself be a form of psychopathy. Or at the very least, grounds for suspicion. In our profession, suspicion of one's colleagues is both endemic and fatal.

The counsellor was a woman in her forties with brittle hair and parallel careers in Tai Chi and small-press poetry. She introduced herself as "Robyn-with-a-y", offered me tea – "Herbal or builder's?" – and invited me to take a seat, or a beanbag if I preferred.

"Not a couch?"

She replied brightly, with admirable forbearance. "I'm a therapeutic counsellor, Robert, not a psychoanalyst."

I felt an involuntary tug raise my eyes to her face. Only Mary called me Robert. When I was a child and Dad came home, every few years, he referred to me as "young man". It started as a joke, I think, when I was five or six, but continued it until I was, indeed, a young man. And then he was dead. My mother had called me "darling", particularly when she found me most irritating.

"So, Robert. You are Robert? Not Bob?"

I closed my eyes.

"Robert. How do you feel?"

"About what?"

"About anything. I want you to be comfortable talking to me about anything at all."

There was a clock in Robyn-with-a-y's consulting room – a cramped spare bedroom without a bed in her small utopian architect's house with its wall-sized windows and efficiently-designed use of space – but it hung on the wall that was now behind me, where she could see it and I could not, which I assumed was no accident. I snuck a peek at my watch. We had another forty-five minutes of this.

"I have a small patch of dry skin," I said.

"Yes?"

"On my thigh. My right thigh. About here."

I scratched my leg through my suit trousers.

"And does it bother you?"

"Sometimes. It comes and goes."

"Have you tried camomile?"

"Tea?"

The woman was so easy to tease I felt sullied.

"Lotion."

I shook my head.

After a while – it felt eternal, but could have been little more than a minute – during which I said nothing and she never once took her eyes off mine, she said, "It is interesting that we have no word for a parent who has lost a child."

Interesting? Only to someone who might actually want people to feel comfortable talking about themselves. I did not reply.

When it was obvious I was not going to pick up the baton, she continued: "A child who loses its parents is an orphan. But a parent who loses his or her child . . . It seems, for us, that is literally unspeakable. Unthinkable, perhaps."

This was easier, I thought, my qualms disappearing in the face of cod semiotics, more fun than talking about myself.

"Isn't it more likely that we have no word precisely because it is – or was, historically – so common?"

She may have heard this response before. Almost before I finished she said, "But we have words for many common things. This chair is common, this carpet . . ."

"Perhaps common wasn't what I meant."

I'd interrupted her in turn. Conversation never flows so well as when it's about nothing.

"Insignificant might be a better word. Meaningless. Something that does not merit comment. A chair is an everyday object, but we still have to refer to it, if we want to make one, or buy one, or" – and here I gave her the sort of smile an interrogator gives when asking a prisoner to indulge him for a moment in some idle speculation – "if you want to invite a visitor to sit down. But you never have to draw attention to the fact of a man having lost a child."

She sipped her tea. "Do you really believe that, Robert?"

"Really," I said, nodding and warming to my theme.

"Having a child doesn't define anyone, the way being an orphan does. If your husband dies, you're a widow; if it's your wife, you're a widower. If I had to guess, I'd say we have these words because widows and widowers have a particular status: they have become re-eligible."

Robyn waited now, evidently expecting further explanation.

"Able to re-marry. A parent whose child dies may still be a parent."

"Or not?"

"Or not. But it's of no consequence to anybody else."

She paused again, but the quality of her waiting seemed subtly different. Not waiting for me to explain, but waiting for the significance of what I had said to sink in. From her posture, from the way she paused after breathing in, catching her lower lip gently with her teeth, it was obvious not only that she didn't agree but that, if I only thought about it, I wouldn't either. Eventually she exhaled and said, "Your wife died, Robert."

"She did. So, yes: I am a widower."

"And you regard yourself as available to re-marry?"

"In theory."

"And you would call yourself a widower?"

"I've never called myself anything of the sort. Not till you started this conversation."

Had she started it? I wasn't sure any more.

"And yet" – she raised a hand slightly as if to forestall an objection I had not made – "even if only when I bring it up, you think of yourself as a widower?"

Did I?

"I suppose so. It's the word we have."

She nodded, then spoke softly, the way people do when

229

they want to insist on something they think you need to hear. "You have also lost a child, Robert."

I thought of Stephen: I had left him, crying, at the nursery. He would get used to it, they'd said, a few weeks earlier, when the arrangement started. So far he hadn't, though, and neither had I. He cried each time I left and, the staff told me – with a note of impatience, of accusation, that strengthened as the weeks went by – he sometimes cried during the day, too. It was not unusual, they said. He would grow out of it. But the look in their eyes said something else.

The counsellor wasn't talking about Stephen, though.

"My wife, Mary" – I hesitated slightly before speaking her name, and then repeated it, indicating that I was taking the counsellor seriously, that I was on the verge of opening myself up – "Mary studied philosophy. She used to quote some gloomy Romanian who said not being born is the best plan of all."

She waited.

"Emil Cioran. He said unfortunately it is within no one's reach – not being born. But it turns out he was wrong. My daughter was fortunate, Ms . . ."

I couldn't remember the woman's surname, and wasn't willing to call her Robyn.

She reached out a hand towards me, apparently involuntarily.

"Do you really believe that, Robert?"

Did I? As much as I believed anything. Which was rather the point.

Had Mary believed it?

I did not answer. Eventually, she said: "There is a word in Hebrew: *horeh shakul.*"

Of course there fucking was. I was only surprised it wasn't a word in Cherokee, or Maori. Unverifiable bullshit so often comes packaged in the trappings of indigenous cultures we've destroyed. I was never happier than the day I discovered the Inuit *don't* have forty-seven words for snow.

"Is that right?"

She nodded. "It denotes a position of honour, of respect, within the community."

She waited again.

I said, "My pregnant wife walked into a bus while I strapped our son into his buggy. I don't see much cause for honour or respect."

There was another silence.

"It was just a thing that happened."

# HE'S BACK

THE MORNING NEWS is not new: a bomb; a small war that has somehow lasted longer than both world wars put together is still not over; an Opposition spokesperson; a dead singer; a rollover on the lottery. I started buying tickets again, sometime after Stephen left home, after the diagnosis, but don't always bother to check the numbers. Now he's back, and the tumour is lithe and sleek within me. Now it really is too late, and winning or not winning seems somehow beside the point.

While Stephen is in the shower, I find a single page beside the typewriter on his desk, a stream of un-spaced numerals, and beside that Stephen's – that is, Mary's – old copy of *City of God*.

I have not seen Warren or visited the Crypt for several years, not even when I was going to the interrogation suite most days, and could easily have stopped off on my way up or down. Even before Stephen left home my visits had become less frequent. As his exams approached, he became busier; after describing his grandfather's death, his journal dried to a trickle, one instalment a week, perhaps, then no more than one a month over his last summer at home. The last of all, written a couple of days before he left for university, was not about his future, about any fears and ambitions he might have had for his new life, but about me. I would be alone; he wondered how well I might cope. Which was kind of him, but hardly necessary. I did not mention it, of course, or respond in any way, even though Warren said I should. I dropped him off outside the college that would be his new home, shook his hand and wished him well.

He had written, sometimes – letters he obviously dashed off hurriedly, between lectures, or between parties, late at night, the upright strokes leaning precipitously to the right, as if in haste to reach the edge of the page, the lines drifting upwards, the blue ink from the fountain pen I'd bought him for his eighteenth birthday smudged by the passage of his hand before it had the chance to dry, giving away much that I had no need to know. Other letters were more considered, the lines straighter, the script formed closer to the perpendicular. These were written in the mornings, I imagined, in the hours of resolution or regret; sometimes they asked for money. At first he bemoaned my lack of email: nobody else wrote letters, he wrote; his new friends thought he was insane. He knew why I didn't use email, of course, although we had never actually discussed the Faculty's security concerns. When his friends asked, he said if he told them that he'd have to kill them. After a while, he wrote, insanity became eccentricity, and the typing, the hand-written letters, the fountain pen he wrote them with all became part of the character he had created for himself, along with the tweed jacket and the horn-rimmed glasses.

It was in one of the late night letters that Stephen wrote about his unborn sister. He wondered how she might have grown up, how they might have grown up together. I'd never answered every letter – it might have created a sense of obligation, a feeling that he could not write again before I had replied – and I didn't answer that one. His next did not mention it.

The point I am making is not that his letters were hand-written but that they were not written in code. Even the late-night ones were plainer, I recall, than the sometimes florid language of the journal: perhaps he'd got all that out of his system? I'd had no need to visit Warren in his chilly laboratory. No reason, either, to summon Warren to my office on the fourth floor, once I had an office of my own. I read the intelligence he decoded. I commissioned research into the cryptographic technologies and techniques being adopted by those of interest to the Faculty in writing, by memorandum. We've had no call to discuss his work, or mine, much less to discuss my son. Now, however, Stephen is home and has begun typing again.

When I arrive, Warren is staring at a huge electronic screen on the wall. It displays a blizzard of purple data points scattered across a graph of incomprehensible regression, dense as grain spilled from a punctured sack. He is wearing the same white coat with its biro marks above the breast pocket, over the same V-neck pullover he always wears in summer; inside the clothes, however, he seems to have shrunk a little. He's older, of course, long past the age when he could reasonably ask the Faculty to let him go. He presses a key on the laptop on the desk in front of him. Up on the screen the cloud of purple data points morphs into an equally incomprehensible cloud of orange data points.

"You see?"

"I see." And possibly I do. If what we in the Faculty do is join the dots – as Gibbon's predecessor, and then Gibbon, always said, and I even found myself saying to Hargreaves when he started – if our job is to spot the patterns in the chaos, then Warren's graph illustrates perfectly why we're barking up the wrong tree. There are just too many dots, and the only pattern is us, making stuff up, telling stories to each other, and to ourselves.

"How's Stephen?" Warren asks.

I am surprised he remembers the name.

"He's back."

The cryptologist expels air through his nose. It might be a snort, or a chuckle, but is too understated to be either.

"I thought he might be."

I hand him the sheet of Stephen's typing, tell him what the source book is. He looks doubtful, or possibly concerned. He doesn't like the fact that Stephen seems to have reverted to the start. I say we shouldn't be surprised when a fig tree brings forth figs, and he takes the sheet of typescript from my outstretched hand without a word.

WHEN BUTLER FIRST allowed me to discover the interrogation suite, and the man in the orange jumpsuit, she said I was to talk to him, and learn to play Go, but I soon found it was not possible to do both at once. That was the first thing I learned from the prisoner. A passing comment on the progress of the game, its mood, its degree of openness or aggression, was possible; a pleasantry about the weather or the passing of the seasons (which he could no longer observe, and about which I could give no concrete information) might be tolerable; but any remark or question that required a more than formulaic response was unthinkable – both impossible to combine with the concentration required, and a desecration of the aesthetics of Go. We would talk and then play, or play and then talk.

The day after meeting B, I let myself into the interrogation room itself, not the observation room, and was immediately distracted by the rank smell I assumed must come from the bucket in the corner, although it was empty. After a moment or two I detected a sweeter undertone of unwashed skin. How quickly we acclimatize.

I began at what I thought was the beginning, and quickly discovered was not.

"Who are you?"

"My name is Volorik."

Volorik. My very own crock of shit. (Simmons' crock of

shit.) I recalled the file photographs. This man was thinner, older: he looked as though someone had draped the skin of a much larger man around his shoulders. Incarceration could do that to anyone, of course. But there was a definite re-semblance. The glasses were similar, although those he wore now were broken, and held together with sellotape. But the Volorik I knew – or, rather, did not know, but had read about; my person of interest, whose flat had been found (albeit by mistake) to contain a veritable arsenal of guns and explosives and a mountain of cash – that Volorik had, according to the files, been handed to the Americans some years ago; what the Americans had done with him was no concern of mine.

"Why are you here?"

He did not seem surprised by the question. When he smiled, the scars fanned out from the corners of his mouth like forest tracks threading through his beard. It looked as if he had been bridled.

"Because you never let me go."

My Volorik had a wife, I recalled – the daughter of a Vis-count – and children. What were their names?

"And why is that?"

"Why?"

"Why do you suppose," I said, speaking as if to someone who did not understand the language well, "that we have never let you leave?"

He laughed, really laughed. Not a bitter, mirthless grin, not a knowing chuckle at the wily innocence of my ques-tion, but a genuine guffaw. I could see the back of his throat, scarlet against the grey skin of his face. When he could speak, he said, "I don't know how familiar you are with my case, Mr . . ."

"Exley."

An interrogator would not have given his name, not even a false one, but I was not an interrogator. He nodded in acknowledgement, assessing, evaluating and filing away the information.

"Mr Exley. If you've read the files, you know just as much as I."

I had read the files; but the files I'd read – and written – closed two years ago.

"Refresh my memory."

He sighed. "I came to this country to bomb a nuclear power station. I came with Brooks and Cable, both originally American – and subsequently also Irish – citizens. I supplied the money, the passports and other documents; they supplied the explosives and weapons. Our controller was Walter Jacobs, an Austrian. I believe – but obviously I can't know – that Jacobs reported directly to Eyquem."

He spoke fluently, as if this were a speech he had rehearsed, but also as if he were really trying not to sound bored as he delivered it. As if he had practised that, too, like an actor, like a politician on the campaign stump.

But what he'd said was nonsense. Brooks and Cable? Jacobs? Eyquem? Hadn't they all been invented by my son?

I said, "Is any of that true?"

"It's all true."

"All of it? Cross your heart and hope to die?"

I said it flatly, letting him know I was aware of both the absurdity and the implicit threat in my words.

His gaze held mine as he said, "It's what it says in your files."

His nose had been broken somewhere along the line, and

had healed crookedly. While his pale eyes locked mine, his face squinted off to my left.

"Because that's what you told us?"

He shrugged. "Because that's what *you* told *me*."

Now, with the benefit of hindsight, I'd like to think it was in that moment that I realized that he had, in fact, answered my earlier question – albeit indirectly, and several steps ahead of me – that he had told me why it was he had never been allowed to go, either to court or to freedom. But, really, I'm not that quick. Mary might have been.

I stood and turned to look at the window between the cell and the observation room through which, just the day before, I had first seen the prisoner – the window I had rightly assumed was not a window, not something he could see through, except, perhaps, on rare occasions when the interrogators' controller thought it appropriate and flicked the switch that cleared the glass. As I had suspected, it was not a blank space or a mirror, but a screen, and, while I was not interrogating Volorik, while he and I were merely conversing, getting to know each other – or rather, he was getting to know me, while I was re-acquainting myself with what I knew of him, comparing what I found to what I remembered from the paperwork – it displayed a constant stream of still photographs and video clips depicting atrocities around the world. Bomb blasts and executions, hostages and funeral pyres and shattered buildings, twisted metal beams and body parts, mass graves in glutinous grey mud, dark fractal stains on bare concrete, fragments of plate glass showering a financial district like lethal ticker-tape, naked prisoners stacked in circus pyramids surrounded by dogs and laughing guards, aeroplanes like fireworks disintegrating in mid-air, forensic records of wounds in which bruised and lacerated flesh became three-dimensional maps of human cruelty, filthy makeshift hospitals where the living died and the dead slept with them. I recognized some of the images – a bomb in a Midlands cinema, a silent death row interview, a beheading, a family with their throats slit in their own kitchen, a bus without a roof. Some were famous, endlessly reproduced around the world, the icons of our faith in news, in our obligation to observe the worst (while rightly suspecting that the worst is being kept from us); others would have been broadcast once and slipped past unremembered, unnoticed; others still, I was sure, like the slaughter of the junior minister and his family, had never been revealed at all. Together they formed the secret capital of the Faculty.

After watching me watch the images for a while, Volorik said: "Eventually they repeat themselves."

I continued watching. "I suppose they must. There must be some limit, even to atrocity."

He said, "I sincerely doubt that. But the interesting thing is, the images keep repeating, some more than others, but there's no pattern. The images repeat, but their order changes. Once in a while, new images are added. I've been watching this slideshow for years now, ever since I first came here. There is no pattern."

I turned away from the screen, back towards the prisoner. I pointed at the low table between us and said, "So what is this game?"

The following morning I ordered up the Volorik files I hadn't read for a couple of years.

LI: *"You are a Muslim?"*
[*Laughter.*]
KV: *"What gave you that idea?"*

SI: *"Call it a shot in the dark."*

[Pause.]

KV: *"An interesting choice of words, don't you think?"*

Asked about the explosives and the guns he'd simply said:

KV: *"Explosives? Guns?"*

LI: *"In your flat, Volorik."*

KV: *"There are no guns or explosives in my flat."*

SI: *"For the tape, the suspect is being shown photographs of guns, knives, and explosives discovered in his flat."*

KV: *"That's not my flat."*

A crock of shit. But whose?

LI: *"Tell me about the Sorbonne, Mr Volorik."*

KV: *"It's a university. In Paris."*

[Pause.]

KV: *"Paris, France."*

SI: *"We know. Speak French, do you?"*

KV: *"It's hard to conduct doctoral research in sign language."*

LI: *"Very good, Volorik. Very . . . droll. Is that the word?"*

KV: *"It's a word, certainly. A French word."*

LI: *"What did you study?"*

KV: [*sighs heavily*] *"Balzac's* Comedie Humaine *and Post-Marxist theories of aesthetics. You'll have found a copy in the apartment."*

[Extended pause.]

I pictured the Lead Interrogator looking up from his notes, allowing the word "Marxist" to settle in the atmosphere of the interrogation room, probably even writing it down, or watching the Second Interrogator write it down, a ponderous sense of having made some breakthrough radiating from their pale, pudgy faces, faces - like my own - that had seen too little daylight.

LI: "Met a lot of old radicals there, did you? Soixante-huitards?"

I was surprised he knew the phrase; I'd only ever heard it from Mary. Of course, appearing stupid was a favourite interrogator's tactic.

[Laughter.]

KV: "I wasn't even born in 1968, Mr . . . Inspector . . . What did you say I should call you?"

The interrogator would not have given his name, or rank.

A crock of shit, then. But there he was. Guilty of something that might have been terrorism, or might have just been over-confidence.

Here he still was.


That afternoon, I said: "How's your wife?"

I tried to say it as if we were two colleagues making conversation over coffee, although no colleague would have asked me that question, obviously, not for almost twenty years. Butler had suggested I visit him in the afternoons – because, I assumed, the interrogations were still in progress, and he would be spending much of each morning strapped to a board tipped back at fifteen or twenty degrees to the horizontal, his head lower than his feet, a wet towel over his face, in a savage parody of a barber's shop, although the razors would be stropped just as loudly, their edges rendered just as sharp, as they nicked his scrotum, while, at a nod from the interrogator, a guard poured more water onto the towel. The water would flood his mouth and nostrils until he drowned, again, and was hauled back to life once more. I wondered how much he resented that diurnal salvation.

He had carefully placed his book aside and risen from

his mattress when I entered the cell. He looked genuinely perplexed.

"My wife?"

"Julia." (I had checked.) "And your children. How old are they now?"

"Do you mean my nephews?"

"Your children, Volorik."

"I have no children. Maybe you're confusing me with my brother?"

Two years of enhanced interrogation seemed to have changed nothing.

"Don't worry, Mr Exley. It happens all the time. We're very alike. We both have beards, although mine is a little longer now, I imagine. We both wear glasses. We even lived in the same apartment block for a while. I would hear him and Julia playing with the boys, or shouting at them. I would hear it through the ceiling – his ceiling, I mean – and would bang on the floor when it got too loud. They lived in the apartment below mine."

# HOW MARY AND I MET

A	T OUR SECOND session, the therapist thanked me
for drawing her attention to Cioran. She had not heard
of him before, she said, and neither had her local librarian.
They had not been sure of the spelling, which had not helped.
But, together, they had found one of his books, and she was
looking forward to reading it, she said, when she had time in
her schedule. Between counselling and Tai Chi and her poetry
(which she must not allow herself *not* to do) it was sometimes
hard to find time to read. She was sure I understood.

She asked how Mary and I met.

"At work."

It was not quite true: I had been working, but Mary had
not known that at the time.

The counsellor must have known, in broad terms at least,
what it meant: the work we did. Despite her flakiness, she
would have been vetted. I wondered how she had come to the
attention of the Faculty. Some friend of a friend, I supposed.
Someone in HR would have shared a gym, a Tai Chi class, or a
mother-and-toddler group with Robyn-with-a-y. Conversation
would have started casually. When the subject of what they
did for work came up, the someone-in-HR would have made
a note – mentally at first, but subsequently written down, at
which point it would have become a concrete possibility. The
note would have been passed up the chain, copied and filed.
Enquiries would have taken place, Robyn's family and friends

traced, her poetry read, and written off, before she would even have been aware she was being considered for a job. More casual meetings would have followed – coffee, a play date with the children, if there were children, a girls' night out – before she'd been invited to meet another friend, a man, one evening, over a glass of wine, perhaps. The man would have been a few years older and, although presentable and friendly, would nonetheless have retained some distance; there would have been something in his eyes that was not altogether present in the bar with them even as he asked if she had ever considered helping her country and she tried not to laugh. They all try not to laugh, which helps. She would have been flattered all the same. The flattery would have piqued her curiosity and, before the evening was over she would have asked herself: "Why not?"

It wasn't hard to imagine the subsequent debate and second thoughts within the office. That poetry? Plato, as Mary always said, would have banned poets for a reason. I could easily imagine it all – the doubts and prevarications of both Robyn and my colleagues, and the eventual triumph of bureaucratic momentum – because, for a while, until shortly before Mary died and I was instructed to attend these counselling sessions, it had been my job. I had been the friend of countless friends with a manner both distant and approachable. That, after all, was how I'd met Mary.

"It's a little weird," she said, the first time we went to bed together, "that you know so much about me. But it also makes it easier."

I knew what she meant. All those facts, those childhood stories, family relations and former lovers we normally ration out so carefully, using them to nurture a growing intimacy and to judge, through the other person's reaction and reciprocation

245

– or lack of reaction or reciprocation – the progress of that intimacy and our own desire to push further ahead, or to draw back while there is still time, all of that I knew about her already. She did not have to tell me anything and, if she did, she knew I'd be unable to resist comparing what she said to the official record, to check for inconsistencies, whether what she said about Aunt Jane tallied with what Aunt Jane herself had said. She did not have to offer anything and yet she knew I was persuaded anyway, or I wouldn't have been there; at the same time, she knew nothing about me beyond my job and was free to ask as much – or as little – as she wished.

That first night, in her flat, when it was already clear that we would sleep together, but neither of us had yet acknowledged it, Mary said, "How did you get into this?"

"My father worked for the Faculty."

She topped up my wine glass, sat beside me on the sofa. "Jobs for the boys?"

"Not exactly. He was a beacon keeper. I was still at university when he died. When I got back to college after the funeral my tutor asked me to meet a friend of his. You can imagine the rest."

She could. It wasn't that long since it had been her.

"How did he die?"

"He slit his stomach open with a hunting knife."

"Oh, God. I'm sorry."

I put my arm around her then.

At work it was clear from the start that she was going to outstrip us all. Gibbon's predecessor, his colleagues and superiors were all keen to exploit her talents and associate themselves with her success; I was pulled along in her slipstream. Our relationship was not secret; we did not discuss our home life in the office or with colleagues, but we each lodged a formal notification with Gibbon's predecessor, who told me I was a lucky man. Relationships between colleagues were actively encouraged within the Faculty – it made life simpler for everyone – but they had to be recorded. I thought our superiors might worry about what would happen once we were no longer colleagues, once, as seemed likely, Mary was elevated to the fourth, fifth and even – who could rule it out? – the sixth floor. Perhaps they thought the vast professional distance between us would simplify matters. More likely, they simply did not believe the relationship would last. When Gibbon's predecessor said I was lucky it was not a benediction.

She was conscious of her talent and had no false modesty. She was beautiful – not just to me: not just in the way men tell themselves their wives or girlfriends are beautiful – but genuinely so. It was a beauty that would last, I thought: she would be beautiful at forty, at sixty, at eighty; a beautiful widow, who would turn from my graveside oblivious to the mourners who wondered why she had wasted such a long and gifted life on me.

"At work?"

Robyn prompted me, neutrally repeating my words.

"I helped recruit her."

"And what drew you to her?"

"She was assigned to me."

"I meant as a person, not a potential recruit. As a woman."

"She . . ."

I hesitated. I could have asked if she'd ever seen a photograph of Mary. But that wasn't the point. The real answer would have involved paddling about in deep and murky pools best left untroubled. Certainly Mary had always had more sense than to try.

I said, "What attracts anyone to anyone? Biology, I suppose."

She waited. She had that part of her technique down pat, I had to give her that.

Eventually I said, "My DNA detected the possibility of replicating itself; it filled my brain with chemicals that shaped my behaviour in such a way as to maximize that possibility."

I smiled to show that even though I was joking she should not assume I did not also believe what I was saying.

"And what about you attracted her?"

Mary said she loved me for my very lack of ambition, which she interpreted as genuine indifference to what I might achieve. We were well matched, she said. I demurred. That's when she first told me about Cioran, about the faculty of indifference. I said indifference might be something I aspired to, but, by aspiring, failed. She laughed. *That*, she said, was why she loved me. She married me, so I had to assume she was to some extent sincere.

"I imagine her DNA detected similar possibilities."

"And you think that's how love works?"

I hadn't mentioned love, and wasn't going to do so now.

"Pretty much."

The remaining sessions followed the same pattern without, as Robyn's report to Gibbon's predecessor put it, any detectable signs of progress. She would invite me to explore my emotions – about Mary's death, about Mary's life, about my own lack of career progression, about our unborn daughter, about Stephen, about my father, about the Faculty – and I would respond with a joke more or less disguised as an interrogation of the question's premise; when she asked why I was joking I would say that I had never been more serious in my life. By the end of each session I left her nowhere to go. Her report concluded that I was in denial, and was inherently unstable. Anger, bargaining and depression would surely follow; the longer and more persistent the denial, the more violent and disruptive the anger would be. I therefore constituted a potential security risk. She recommended that I be suspended from active investigations.

Gibbon's predecessor read the report but ignored the recommendation. He completed a form, signing the box that confirmed I had undertaken therapeutic counselling and appended the counsellor's report without further comment. There was no shortage of work, no shortage of real threats to contain. The team was already a man down, its best man (even if she were a woman). It would struggle in ways that would not reflect well on its Divisional Director, even without losing another steady worker. Where would he find *two* new operatives? And the plain fact was that I *was* stable. In the six months after Mary's death, my work simply continued, neither improving nor – despite the practical implications of suddenly having to bring up Stephen on my own – noticeably deteriorating. Nothing changed; nothing happened.

So nothing happened, but it had been a close shave.

When, fifteen years later, I learned that some portion of my DNA had after all found its own way to replicate itself, and was doing so with astonishing speed deep within my gut, I had no desire to repeat the experience. This time there was no possibility that nothing would change.

# FOUR

# THE ENDGAME

REUSING AN OLD source book, Warren's algorithms are able to decode Stephen's journal on the spot. He reads it coming off the printer, hands it to me and says, "Have you really never heard it?"

Stephen left the book right there, beside the typewriter, as if to remind me, after all this time, to make my task easier, to make sure I cannot avoid discovering what's on his mind, but will not – given the circumstances – be able to discuss it with him. He has begun to write to me again in code, after several years, and what he has chosen to write about is the knocking on the walls of our family home. The knocking I have never heard.

When I leave the Crypt, I continue downwards. There is no uncertainty, now, about my directions, no danger that I might turn right where I should go right on, or vice versa. I have been coming here almost daily, several times a week, for several years: I am free not to think about where to place my feet, which corner to pass, which door to open or not open, but about the sealed play I left in Volorik's cell yesterday.

We started our latest game almost three weeks ago. The middle phase, which is always the most intense, and which demands the highest concentration, is almost over: we will soon be entering the endgame. The pace will pick up. Of our allotted hours, I have three remaining, Volorik less than one. Normally, this would give me no real advantage. In previous games I have watched him take two or three hours to make a single play, extending our sessions way beyond their allotted times – keeping me there, three or four floors below ground level while my colleagues gathered in the Lamb & Flag – and then go on to storm through the endgame, placing a hundred stones in a matter of minutes, playing out the consequences of his earlier moves, and of my failure adequately to counter them, overwhelming me with a relentless, machine-gun rapidity of movement that defied the eye, let alone the brain. This time, however, when he opens the envelope, slides out the chart and looks for my latest play, he will not find it to begin with. It will be nowhere near the skirmishing that filled much of yesterday's session, nowhere he might anticipate. It will take him a moment or two to find it; and then, I foresee – I hope – he will be astounded. I am looking forward to that moment.

As usual, in this game I've spent three weeks gradually losing – staking out territory, peeping into his, but all the time watching, with each White response, the balance tilt remorselessly in his favour. But just before it was again finally too late, I spotted a sliver of opportunity. With my penultimate move (a well disguised mistake) I bought a little time, the space of a single play, with which to make my bold and dangerous challenge.

It is an audacious move, cutting deep into territory he has not fully secured (which would normally be a task for the endgame) but which he must nonetheless be counting as his own. He will see at once that my challenge might be worth a dozen points, if I can hold my nerve during the battle to follow – enough to turn the game around. But the beauty of it is that it is so outrageous, so unconventional, that he will have to spend long enough calculating a response for even him to feel the pressure of the sand running through the hourglass. And in that pressure, for the first time ever, lies my chance of winning.

It was an act of gamesmanship – of which, in retrospect, I am both childishly proud and a little ashamed – to time my play to be the last of the day, sealed, and not revealed until the following afternoon, so that I could spend the night, and this morning, in anticipation, while Volorik has no idea what is about to happen, is a little complacent perhaps that the thickening white lines have become impregnable and that he will soon, once again, rush through the final moves of my defeat.

As I make my way down from the Crypt, I find that I am not indifferent.

In his cell, Volorik is already kneeling at the board, studying again the disposition of the stones. He eats little of the food the guards continue to bring him every day, and yet, in the years I have been visiting, he has grown no thinner, merely denser, more concentrated, within his loose and outsized skin, his teeth too large for his mouth. He has the predator's natural ability to switch instantly from sprawling inattention to easy, practised savagery. When I arrive he is reabsorbing the board with an intensity that could split atoms.

So much for complacency. It was never a realistic expectation. But still, he can have no inkling of what is about to be revealed.

Gesturing at the board, he asks whether I prefer to talk first, then play; or play, then talk. As I have said, it is not possible to do both at once.

Wishing to prolong the moment, I say: "Duty first."

He relaxes, uncoils a little. "What would you like to talk about today?"

I talk about my son.

I say, "He seems to think the knocking is some kind of message, a signal."

Volorik regards me evenly, fingering the strap of his flip-flop where it separates the big toe of his right foot from the other toes. "Could he be right?"

Could he?

I have spent my working life at the Faculty convinced there is no signal, only noise. Here there isn't even noise.

"There is no knocking. How can that be a signal?"

# THE VOLORIK I'D MET

WHEN I ASKED about his children, the Volorik I'd then met only twice asked me to believe that he was not the Volorik whose flat the Faculty had raided in error some years earlier, not the Volorik whose flat had nonetheless been filled with weapons and explosives and cash, along with a wife and two young boys, but was, in fact, his brother, the target of the surveillance I had ordered, the occupant of the flat I had given instructions to be raided. He said he had lived there with a woman – the woman, I remembered, after leaving his cell for the second time, who spoke to the TV news and might, perhaps, have winked into the camera. Who was she? Volorik had not explicitly denied being married, I realized; he had denied only having children. In my surprise I had not immediately sought to clarify the point.

I returned to my office. Bernadette said I looked tired. She offered to make tea and reminded me the monthly status report was due by the end of the day. I thanked her. She said I'd have to get it done by four-thirty if I wanted her to type it up; it was Friday and she had to leave promptly to visit her mother-in-law that weekend. I said I would do my best.

Could there really be two Voloriks? It is a curious quirk, long since drilled into us by the Faculty, that terrorism seems to attract a higher proportion of literal brothers in arms than one would expect from any random sample of merely violent men. The finding was statistically significant. In the United

States, in France, Belgium, Ireland and Britain, in Chechnya, Ukraine, Uzbekistan, Sudan, Somalia and all across West Africa, in Afghanistan, Iraq, Syria and Turkey, in Morocco, Canada, Colombia, Mexico, Punjab, Peru, Sri Lanka, the Philippines and who knew where else besides, in market places, shopping centres, schools, concert halls and sports stadiums, in churches, mosques and synagogues, on beaches, trains, buses, ships and aeroplanes, anywhere that people gathered, anywhere the sheer crush of humanity might maximize the efficient butchery of flesh, sibling teams had executed numberless atrocities. So, yes, it was certainly plausible that there might be more than one Volorik, and that they might be brothers. If there were two of them it was not inconceivable – indeed, some case studies suggested it was even likely – that they might live close to each other, might even share a house. But no degree of statistical probability could tell me if it was the case, *in this case.*

I went back over the other things he'd told me the day before. Apart from the rules of Go, there had not been much. In his well-rehearsed confession, his summary of why he was there, in the Faculty, shackled to the cement floor of a cell three or four floors below ground level, he had named names: Cable, Brooks, Jacobs, Eyquem. Names I knew, of course, but there had been no mention of a second Volorik. So who had planned to destroy the nuclear power plant? Volorik or his brother? If it were his brother's flat we had raided, his brother we had detained, where was he? And why was *this* Volorik here, in the Faculty's basement, telling me he was guilty but it wasn't him I'd caught, two or three years ago, with a flat full of explosives and guns and money?

I looked up at the clock on the wall; I had little more than half an hour to complete my report. Beside the clock hung the picture I'd ordered to replace *Las Meninas*, the picture of a jug, a string of pearls, a dagger in a decorated sheath, the hilt carved into the shape of a horse's head. The jug was nothing but an orange outline, the pearls draped from its handle made to appear spherical by a simple spot of white on each, the dagger touching neither, existing in a different plane, rendered flat, with impossible perspective, unconnected to the life of the still life, but, in consequence, impossible to ignore.

I opened a desk drawer – the second drawer, not the one I'd opened when this had been Gibbon's desk and I'd found the tube of moisturiser identical to the one Butler had given me. There was still moisturiser there. Not the same tube of course, but one just like it, the same brand, because promotion and a change of office had done nothing to relieve the dry skin and the itching, and even though, by then – when I'd begun to visit Volorik – I knew that dry skin was the least of my problems, in relation to my health, that is, I had nonetheless used up the moisturiser that had been Gibbon's, and had replaced it more than once. I had also found, in passing, that the wooden desk was less effective for scratching my thighs against than the olive metal desks in the third-floor offices, although less likely, it turned out, to rip my trousers; there were always swings and roundabouts.

I opened the second drawer and pulled out a blank report pro forma. I completed it quickly, summarizing the sit reps I'd received from Simmons, Leach, Hargreaves and even Butler – even though we both knew by then that Butler was not my junior, not my direct report, but my Director, or she was somehow both. The fiction that she was merely a member of the team still had to be maintained, so I incorporated her reports to me in my report to her. I did not mention Volorik, however, even though I knew she knew about him. It was too soon and, besides, although she had not said so, I had the feeling that his presence in the building and anything I might discuss with him or learn from him, not excluding the rules of Go, were matters I should not commit to paper.

I stood and left my office, dropping my completed draft on Bernadette's desk as I passed. I would leave early, too.

It was a pleasant, late spring afternoon and the breeze coming off the river felt soft on my face. From time to time it stirred the litter and the fallen cherry blossom on the embankment. I decided to skip the Lamb & Flag and walk home. There was no need to do so: there were for once no bombs, no threats, and as far as I knew the trains were running normally. But I also had no need to hurry. I had time. It was early and, in any case, there was no one waiting for me.

As I passed the railway station, my rhythm settled and I recalled the time, before Stephen left home, when I'd made this walk out of necessity. It had been raining then, or drizzling at least, and I had worn an overcoat. Despite the miserable December weather, I had become too hot. I'd removed my coat and carried it slung across my shoulder, the strap cutting off the circulation in my fingers; even so, I had begun to sweat. The sweat irritated the patches of itchy skin on my thighs, around my waist, where the clothes rubbed. But, more than that, I recalled feeling the first stabbing pains, far more than a simple itch, that turned out to be not just haemorrhoids – which would have been, frankly, insupportable – but cancer of the bowel, which, as it turns out, I have been able to support, at least until now, today, when I have written two or three dozen more monthly reports, not one of which mentions Volorik, and I am on the verge of beating him, for the very first time, in a game of Go. I can feel it, dense and slippery. It keeps me company as it presses against my belly just above my pelvic bone; I imagine it sleek, contained, shrouded in a slick, translucent caul, eyes veiled, like an unborn creature, biding its time. Sometimes, though, it turns on me – savage and ferocious, its teeth and claws tearing at my flesh, our flesh.

Away from the river, beside the busy road, the breeze became imperceptible and, although it was spring and I had no coat, I quickly became too hot again, and began to sweat. I loosened my tie, undid the top button of my shirt. I took off my suit jacket and hung it over my shoulder as I had, on that earlier occasion, my overcoat. The pain in my abdomen was what I then regarded as mild-to-moderate – four out of ten: I have since recalibrated my perceptions more than once – and I thought walking five miles would be no problem, and might do me some good. The tumour then would have been no larger than my thumb.

As the road broadened and I approached the bus shelter where, previously, two men had blocked my path, I recalled the voice of the man who had subsequently rung to ask me about them. He had not given his name. I'd assumed at the time he was from the fifth floor, a bag-carrier to one of the Directors. Had Butler been a Director even then? Had the man with the smooth voice been working for her? Had the whole thing been part of some selection process of which I had been unaware? It seemed unlikely; I could only say that I heard nothing more about the men I'd injured, and that I was promoted. Were these two facts connected? I have connected them now merely by raising the question, by linking them together in a single sentence. But does that constitute a pattern? A story? I can't say.

I wondered if the vicious knife I took from one of the men might still be there, on the roof of the bus shelter, where I'd lobbed it two or three years before: probably not. More likely, it had been found by some excited teenager, climbing onto the shelter to demonstrate his own testosterone; or spotted in advance, perhaps, from a window high up in the flats behind the wall, and recovered with premeditated intent. Perhaps it had already been used again, in attack or defence, had already pierced flesh, severed arteries, and left its victims face down, bleeding life into the gutter; or perhaps it had not been found, or used, at all. I would never know. There was no one waiting for a bus this time, or pretending to wait for a bus, and I continued unimpeded.

Walking home, I would not pass the corner where the cherry tree leaned out from the pavement at forty-five degrees, the tree I passed most days, when I came home by train and walked up from the station. I would not be reminded of the lottery and prompted to wonder what I would do if I ever won, even though I had by then begun buying tickets again, knowing it was already too late, and did not always check the numbers.

I let myself into the empty house and poured myself a glass of wine. It was a Friday evening and, quite possibly, I would not have to speak to anyone for more than forty-eight hours.

I STILL HAVE not won the lottery – or, if I have, I haven't
noticed.

When I returned to the interrogation room the following
Monday, I asked Volorik about Butler. I don't know why. I
hadn't meant to. I'd planned to ask more about his supposed
brother, and his brother's family, about the flats they'd lived
in, one above the other, Volorik – *my* Volorik, as it were, the
one I would be asking – in the flat above his brother and his
brother's wife and children, and about the woman he shared
his own flat with, the woman I had seen on the television once,
who had said she thought her neighbours a nice family who
didn't look the type, the woman, I thought, knowing that it
could not be true, who had winked at the camera, at me, as
she spoke. Instead, I asked about Butler, a breach of protocol
greater even than revealing my own name.

If Volorik was surprised, he didn't show it. He considered
the question briefly, before saying: "She is very competent, I
think. Professional."

I waited, not knowing what to do with this answer, since
I didn't really know why I'd asked the question.

"She is respected by her staff, I think?"

I nodded, as if Volorik were confirming something I'd
suspected.

"I like her."

"You like her?"

"When she orders any enhancement of my interrogation, she has the humanity to be present herself. To witness the increase in my pain."

An interesting definition of humanity, as Mary might have said, but not necessarily inaccurate.

"How do you know Butler gives the orders?"

He looked up at me. "Because she has the decency to tell me so."

I had ordered nothing, had been in no way responsible for his interrogation – had been only accidentally involved in his original arrest – but something about the way he said this, or perhaps about the way I had remained standing, while he knelt behind the low Go table, made the words feel critical, as if I were already falling short of some standard I had not been aware existed.

In retaliation, I suppose, I asked about the defence minister, about his wife and children and the nanny, and about the married couple who had killed them. I described Butler's intense, but functional reaction to the incident. Her brief display of revulsion and guilt, her threat of resignation: it all served a purpose for Butler herself, I said, however little it achieved for the participants, who were, of course, all dead.

"The couple were called Rachel and Peter Slater." He spoke in the same fluent, practised tone in which, the previous week, he had answered my questions about why he was there. "I recruited them, under instruction from Eyquem via Jacobs. Brooks supplied the suicide vests. Rachel Slater was an architect, her husband a lawyer. They had been married twelve years; they were church wardens, volunteers at their local food bank and homeless shelter where, with his wife's cooperation, Peter Slater had been abusing vulnerable girls for almost a decade."

It was outlandish; it was possible. (It was also possible that neither Peter nor Rachel Slater had ever existed.) "Is that true?"

He did not answer immediately. Instead, he seemed to be undertaking some assessment, performing some calculation in his head. His broken nose pointed straight up at me. Eventually he asked, "What month is this?"

"You know I can't tell you that."

Any more than I could tell him where the name Rachel Slater came from, or Brooks, or Eyquem. Any more than I could tell him my name, or Butler's.

He was polite, nonetheless. "Not even what season?"

I shook my head.

He acquiesced, not without some show of good humour – a sigh, a shrug, eyebrows raised above the rim of his spectacles – to indicate that he knew the score and it was not, after all, the end of the world. "Then you will forgive me if I cannot be precise, but for several years I have been telling your colleagues what I could."

"Why?"

He did not appear surprised by the question.

"Because I had no choice. But that's not my point. I'm not trying to exculpate myself, not trying to suggest I have been a model prisoner."

"You cooperated to avoid torture?"

Another breach of protocol on my part. Torture was not a word articulated within the Faculty.

He shook his head: I had a lot to learn. "I have cooperated *and* been tortured. There was no alternative to either."

Throughout this conversation he had been kneeling at the Go board as if to signal – albeit patiently, with no suggestion in his words or gestures that his mind was focussed on anything but answering my questions – that perhaps the real business of the afternoon might begin. When I asked why he thought there was no alternative, however, he rose as far as the chain on his wrist would allow, scooted in a semi-circle to his mattress and picked up the fat black paperback *City of God* I had noticed the first time I saw him, the previous week, from the observation room next door. Much like Stephen's copy – which had been Mary's copy – the spine was almost white with the tracery of cracks where he had held the book open, perhaps pressing it flat against the mattress or the concrete floor; many pages were folded down at the corners. Nonetheless, he flipped quickly to a page four-fifths of the way through. He returned to the centre of the room, facing me across the low Go table.

He ran his finger down the text. "Augustine says we torture not because we know the accused has committed a crime, but because we cannot be certain he has not. We want to eliminate that doubt, if at all possible, in order to avoid executing an innocent man."

"We don't execute anyone. And you confessed."

"I agreed."

"You planned to bomb a nuclear power plant. You told me so yourself."

He nodded. "Everything the Faculty said I did, I said I did. Which just guaranteed that you would torture me more."

I could not admit that I might have understood.

He smiled and gestured broadly with his left, unshackled hand. "Sit down, Mr Exley. Make yourself comfortable. We may not have much time for Go today, but we shall see."

I sat, awkwardly, on the floor, not quite knowing what to do with my legs; I could not sit on them, as Volorik did.

"When you're being tortured, Mr Exley – or rather, when you have been tortured, and find yourself in the interval between having been tortured and waiting to be tortured again, *in the present* that is, in the moment between the past and the future, between the memory of pain and the anticipation of future, always greater pain – at that moment, it is not possible *not* to talk." He patted the book beside him.

I had a feeling Mary might have told me this before, if only I could remember what she'd said.

"Augustine says time has three principal tenses: past, present, future. In this it is like language, which is naturally no coincidence. The three tenses coexist in the mind, Mr Exley, and in speech. The past exists only in memory, the future in anticipation: but memory and anticipation themselves exist only in the present of the one remembering, the one anticipating. When we speak of the past, or of the future, we do so in the present."

He paused, as if to confirm that I was following so far, to give me the opportunity to interrupt, to seek clarification. I said nothing. Mary *had* told me this, possibly the first time we met, before she knew why we'd met.

"He also says we know three things about ourselves: that we exist, that we know that we exist, and that we are glad of it. We can no more wish not to exist than we can wish not to be happy, for existence is a pre-condition of happiness."

I remembered now. Mary had told me this, too, that we existed, that we knew we existed. She had not said anything about happiness.

I said, "Who's happy? I don't think happiness has anything to do with it."

"In the city of man, I grant you, true happiness is not possible. We exist, but we cannot live as we wish, because we know that we are going to die. Without the grace of God there can be no hope of eternal felicity."

"Bollocks."

"Excuse me?"

"That's bollocks. Plenty of people choose not to be happy. Not to exist. The Slaters, for example."

"Or your father?"

I was startled.

I shouldn't have been. How had he known about my father's suicide? The same way he knew the name Eyquem; the way he knew about Cable and Brooks and the Slaters; the way he knew his own name was Volorik. Because we'd told him. Because he'd told us. Stephen had written the story down, encrypted it, and I had passed it on to be decoded. I'd treated Warren as if our transactions were personal, discrete, unrelated to our professional duties: as if such a thing were possible. I'd requested a favour, Warren had apparently obliged; the only price seemed to be his desire to take an interest in my son, to advise me about Stephen's welfare. I realize now, with embarrassment, that I'd taken even that as an attempt at friendship. What on earth had given me that impression? When Stephen left home I stopped visiting the Crypt.

I said, "Or my father."

"Your father only wished not to exist in the future. Not in the past, not to have not existed, and not even in the present, because he had to exist to form the wish."

Which was exactly the sort of thing I couldn't take when Mary or Stephen tried to explain philosophy to me.

"You're splitting hairs. My father certainly anticipated his future in his present. He took a knife in his present and slit his belly open. He watched, in his present, while his organs slipped out and pooled around his feet."

How did I know that? The same way Volorik did: from Stephen. Or, rather, from Warren. From the Faculty.

I realized I had no way of knowing how much of the journal that I'd read had been written by my son, how much by my employers. By Volorik.

That was when he told me about *seppuku*, about *harakiri*. After which he said, "Didn't it ever strike you as odd that when Rachel Slater told the defence minister's family to slit each other's throats, they did?"

I thought he was changing the subject, and said so.

"Didn't you at least wonder why none of them refused, even when it was obvious that cooperating would not save their own lives?"

I said nothing.

"I suppose it's possible. Conceivable. Some Greek tragedy in shorthand. But it's not very likely, is it?"

"I don't know."

"You don't know?"

I didn't answer. When, after a few moments, Volorik spoke again, it seemed to me that he was changing tack once more. I had only known him a few days, then, and had not yet become accustomed to the feints, diversions and counter-thrusts by which he gradually pieced together his arguments – or, indeed, his games – coordinating apparently unrelated strands until, eventually, the net was pulled together.

"The suicide and the victim of torture might be extreme cases," he said, "but they're by no means exceptional. Perhaps they can best be considered as thought experiments, in which the conditions of human existence are simplified to the point where superficial complexity and irrelevant distractions fall away."

"And the truth can be revealed?"

My tone was sarcastic. Volorik acknowledged the interruption, but continued unruffled.

"Just so. But not of course the truth the torturer seeks. That, after all, is among the first of the irrelevant details to be discarded."

"So you lied?"

Volorik sighed heavily. He closed his eyes, as if disappointed, then made an effort to rally himself.

"As I've already said, I told you what you told me. What else could I do? I knew nothing else. I presume it was true, although obviously I have no way of knowing and, in any case, the question is of no importance. For the tortured the only thing that matters is to keep talking, to keep expanding the present, to keep forestalling a future that we fear will be worse even than the past. That fear *is* our present; our only wish is to prolong it as far as possible. We choose to live in fear – for fear of something worse. In this, like I say, those of us who have been tortured, who are going to be tortured, are no different from the great mass of humanity. It's just that our imperative is clearer." He smiled as he spoke, shook his head fractionally. "Occam's isn't the only razor that simplifies."

He paused again. It looked as if he might have finished. He had explained why he confessed – although *confess* was too simple a word for what he had described – but hadn't yet explained why that confession necessarily led to further torture.

"I understand, I think. When you were asked what you knew about X, you told us about X. The Slaters, for example. We asked whether you recruited the Slaters. We had previously asked what orders you had received from Eyquem. So now you told us Eyquem ordered you to recruit the Slaters. Am I right?"

"More or less."

"You vomited back up what we fed you?"

He nodded. "Sometimes, in the early days, I tried to embellish my stories, I tried to add a little colour. To incriminate new people, maybe innocent people. The defence minister's family, for example. I thought it might please my interrogators, make me more credible. I quickly found it had the opposite effect. When I invented details, or even when I offered truths they were not aware of, they could not corroborate them. My facts did not coincide with those in their files. I must be lying, so they increased my torture. The purpose of torture, remember, is to remove the torturer's doubt about the possible innocence of his victim. And the only way I could avoid doubt was to repeat what my torturers told me, at ever-greater length, but without additional invention. It has not been easy."

"But it made you guilty?"

"And ensured my further torture. If I knew so much, what more did I know?"

I said, "So now I know your secret. Why are you telling me this?"

He laughed – the laugh of an indulgent parent whose child considers himself unique. I saw the scars again, around his mouth. He said, "Do you imagine your colleagues don't already know this? Ms Butler, for example. Brigid. Do you think she doesn't know?"

"Then why is she still torturing you?"

"Because in the city of man, Mr Exley, you can't avoid ignorance. The torturer cannot know for sure that I am not innocent, at least of the crimes I'm accused of. But unfortunately, as Augustine also says, the exigencies of human society make judgment also unavoidable. She cannot know, but she has to know. You have to know, but you cannot know. And there you have it."

He sounded so certain of our ignorance, so practised and so fluent, exactly as he had when he told me about the Slaters, or that Eyquem had ordered Jacobs to order him to bomb a nuclear power plant. But something did not ring true, something more than the simple fact that my father wasn't called Eyquem, even if Eyquem was a code name.

I said, "That may have been true in Augustine's day."

"Do you think our relation to the truth and judgment changes over time? Do you think torture has progressed that much in sixteen centuries?"

I waved that away. "I don't think we care about the truth. I don't think it matters a fig to the Faculty whether you're guilty or not. We're not interested in judgment, or even punishment. What matters is that you exist."

Volorik nodded, considering what I had said, but without surprise.

"And why is that?"

I saw belatedly where he'd been leading me. I said, "The Faculty exists because you exist. It can't put you on trial because everything you know, we told you, and you told us. To find you guilty would prove nothing; to find you innocent would prove nothing. We can't set you free, because you know everything. If we kill you we would simply have to reinvent you, to find a second Volorik - or indeed a third. So what can we do?"

"Can't you see?"

My question had been rhetorical; his wasn't. I couldn't see.

"You can make me your Director-General."

This time, I laughed. "Is that a job application?"

He watched me for a while and I had the sense, again, that he was calculating, assessing options, reviewing his past knowledge of me and anticipating my future. Eventually he said, "Perhaps there is time for a little Go after all?"

As we played, this time on a grid thirteen points by thirteen, I found myself - while waiting for his moves and appearing to consider my own - thinking instead about what he had said. He'd sounded both intense and relaxed, as if he knew what he was saying inside out, as if he had no doubt, either of his own views or of his right to lay them out before me, but also as if he were taking the conversation seriously: that he was repeating something he had thought and said a hundred times before made it no less important or true. It was a skill he had honed with the strongest incentive over several years. But then he'd capped it off with that joke about being the D-G.

"Mr Exley?"

He could see my mind had wandered from the game.

"I'm sorry."

I looked at the board, but could not remember which had been his last play. I placed a black stone randomly in an otherwise unoccupied corner of the grid, and he considered it seriously.

It had surely been a joke?

He'd said suicides and torture victims were extreme but not special cases. His argument concerned only the prolongation of an intolerable present for fear of – in the certainty of – an even more intolerable future. When you reduced life to that dilemma, was it possible to remain indifferent? Was one not forced to live as if life might not be intolerable, forced to hope that it might even be improved? Had that been what Mary meant by living as if it made a difference?

Apparently ignoring my last move, he placed a white stone alongside a group where we had previously been tussling irresolutely.

I said, "What about the Slaters? What about my father? As far as I can see, you've only explained why we don't all kill ourselves – not why so many of us do."

Volorik placed a finger on a point next to his last stone. "Play here. I want to show you something."

I did as he asked. He responded with another white stone and, again, indicated my next move. After we had repeated this two or three more times he leaned back, holding his hands with the palms up, the chain rattling at his right wrist.

"You see?"

I looked at the corner of the board where we had been playing. I saw white stones and black stones, nothing more. The previous week, he'd explained how territory that might appear secure was not, unless it contained at least two "eyes" – that is, points the other player could not occupy – within a group; such stones were said to be "alive", while those which remained on the board but lacked the security of two eyes – and which would therefore eventually, inevitably, be captured

– were "dead". Hard as I looked now I could not detect any of the patterns he had shown me. I could not make sense of the stones he had made me lay, could not see which were dead and which, if any, were alive.

I shook my head. "I can't see who is going to win this."

"That's what I wanted to show you. This situation occurs from time to time. In Japanese it is called *seki*. The word is sometimes translated as "mutual life" but in reality it is a situation in which there is neither life nor death."

Only much later, recalling our conversation for Butler's benefit, did I realize he had not been joking after all.

Now, when he fetches the envelope and opens my sealed play, kneeling at his side of the board, while I stand, looking down at him, it is exactly as I have hoped it might be.

Today, this afternoon, will be different.

For a moment, more than a moment, he is perplexed. He looks up from the chart as if to ask why I have made no play. I smile, gesturing with my eyes, with my chin, that he should look again. He does, and when, after several moments more, he finds the spot marked Black 132 he gasps, or rather cries, a sharp sound of real pain. He closes his eyes and keeps them closed as I lower myself awkwardly to the floor. (I have tried over the years to sit on my heels as Volorik does, but the pain in my tendons is unbearable.) He does not watch as I pick a black stone from the pot on my side of the low table, holding it delicately between my first and index fingers, as I have seen him do, and place it on the point marked on the chart. At the click of the stone on the wooden board he lets out a soft grunt. After that he says nothing, makes no sound, for thirty-four minutes. His response, when it comes, surprises me in turn. White 133 is neither defence nor counter-attack as such, but rather a distraction, a sub-plot, a play in another quarter altogether. It is a move I cannot ignore and to which I now have to respond, one which we both knew would have to be played at some point, but which we both expected to leave until later, until the endgame. We each play our next six stones briskly, automatically, there being no real choice but to work out the consequences until he has secured the territory that was always going to be his, and I have limited the damage. He picks my captured stones from the board in silence. I respond provocatively, placing another stone diagonally alongside Black 132, reinforcing the unorthodox assault of my sealed play from the day before. This he appears to ignore, using his own move to open up another diversionary front, aimed at limiting my gains in the bottom left-hand corner of the grid, gains and limits that we have both discounted already in our calculations, and which will therefore, short of some suicidal failure of judgment on either side, have no bearing on the outcome of the game. Nonetheless, the moves are trickier, at least for me. While he plays his next four stones in less than a minute, I use up twenty. He hesitates, though, over the final move in the sequence, delaying it unnecessarily until the hour is up and then declaring mildly that his next move will be the sealed play that ends the day's session. It is the first time he has spoken since opening the envelope an hour earlier. I agree and, although there can be no doubt what the move will be, stand and step away from the table, allowing him to mark the chart secretly, to slide it into a fresh envelope. He seals and signs the envelope, passing it to me to countersign.

He has said nothing about the move with which I ended the previous session and started this. He has not responded directly to it, or even acknowledged it has happened, except in that short involuntary cry of pain and the soft grunt that followed. In Go, Volorik is my teacher, my mentor. I didn't expect him to take the possibility of losing so badly. Is not this breakthrough, this improvement in my game, the most sincere compliment I can make to the skill with which he has nurtured me? I expected surprise, but not this sullen truculence. I expected, to be honest, some congratulation, some admiration for my audacity. I expected a counter-attack the equal of the move I'd made. Instead, he has played for time, when he has almost no time left. He has played out the session, giving himself twenty-four hours to consider his real response. It is gamesmanship, I conclude, worse than my own mild transgression in making the attack a sealed play; it is a tactic he has always condemned as unworthy of the ideals of Go and those who play it.

He has said nothing.

"**H**OW WAS YOUR day?"

Stephen turns from the cooker, surprised. I've said it before he can.

I press home my advantage: "What have you been up to?"

I have been at work. I've fought my way to the centre of the city on a crowded, sweaty train and earned the money to buy the food that Stephen is now cooking. From the sweltering airless confines of my fourth floor office, with its heavily-curtained window I cannot open whatever the weather, I descended to the air-conditioned, season-free interrogation suite, where I talked about Stephen before teetering on the brink of beating Volorik at Go – which, for the last few years, has been most of my job. He span it out, but tomorrow afternoon, when I return, he will have no real response to my unorthodox attack and he will lose.

I will have won.

Then what?

I also have a tumour I can feel through my belly, when it's sleeping, like a misplaced baby. When it wakes, it shoots pain I can no longer begin to measure through my body: pain that, lately, has begun to blot out everything in its path – sight, sound, thought, sensation – until it fills the universe with its howling, irrefutable demands, before subsiding once again, beating out pulses of merely bearable discomfort and nausea, which spread and slow and deepen as they ripple out from my intestines to the far points of my body and I know that it – the pain – will come again, come harder, soon, but not now; and for some minutes, or hours, or days there is nothing but the memory of pain, the anticipation of more pain.

I live in the present, now, Stephen in his own past. He has returned home. But what now? What next?

He has joked about joining the Faculty. But what else is there?

He says, "I've been playing my cello."

"That's good."

"And I've worked out how to stop the knocking."

The knocking I have never heard.

"Good."

After dinner we watch the television news. The beach of a popular holiday resort has been strafed with machine-gun fire by a twin-engine plane that subsequently crashed into a luxury hotel. An international summit of forty-seven heads of state has reached deadlock. Markets in London and New York have risen by a fraction of one per cent. Tomorrow's weather will be hotter than today's, with a high risk of thundery showers in the south.

Stephen retires to his room. I hear the dull thwack of the typewriter's arms against fresh paper.

I fall asleep on the sofa with the television on.

Hours later, possibly – it may be much less – I wake to a film I soon realize I've seen before: more than twenty years ago, in the cinema, with Mary. It's a comedy, and hasn't dated well. I switch it off and go to bed.

In the morning there is a sheet of paper on the kitchen table, filled with the familiar stream of numerals. In the past Stephen always maintained the pretence that his journal was private, that I would not, could not, read it. Something has changed, some ripple disrupting the endless, infinite repetition of pain and not-pain. Something will happen, if only I live long enough to see it.

When I leave for work in the morning, taking the typed sheet with me, Stephen has not come down from his room.

# METASTASIS

# HOW WILL IT BE TODAY?

WHEN VOLORIK HANDS me the sealed envelope that contains his last move from yesterday, I ask if I really need to open it, the move being so obvious, there being no choice, the interesting play being not this one but his next, in which he will finally have to respond to my breakthrough, and we will reach the point where I may even win.

I am excited; there is no avoiding it. Such lack of indifference does not make me a murderer.

"Open it," he says, facing me squarely with his broken nose while the eyes behind his spectacles slide somewhere to my right.

I take the envelope. It has been opened and re-sealed since I counter-signed it. I hold it up to show that I have noticed.

"Open it," he says again.

I slip the chart out and unfold it. A vast black stain, doubled and blotted like a Rorschach test, obscures all but the most peripheral points on the grid. A huge belch of pain radiates from my bowels, knocking the air out of my lungs. Coincidence, I swear. I've lived with my tumour – it has lived with me – long enough to know. We depend upon each other, sustain each other, but there is no connection, no pattern to draw between its behaviour and my mood. I cannot wish it away; I cannot accelerate its growth. It is me, but it will grow and reproduce itself in its own good time, it will propagate our DNA the best way it knows how.

I have tried not to live as if there were anything I could do about it.

But the agony has never been this bad. I stagger and sit heavily beside the Go table, knocking over the pot of black stones, scattering them across the floor. It looks as if ink has sprayed off the chart and over the interrogation cell. I surf the crest of a wave of pain, desperate not to fall in too deep. I am incapable of speech, even if I knew what to say.

Volorik says, "Go is not just a competition. We were creating something delicate and beautiful. A painting, a watercolour. You have defaced it."

I hold the chart up weakly. It's as close as I can get to saying: me? You think *I'm* the one defacing things?

"In painting there is no rule that says you can't punch a hole through the middle of the canvas, but almost no one does."

I feel as if I'm going to vomit; it is a very real possibility.

"You, however, you have smashed your fist through our game for no other reason than to win."

When the pain subsides enough to let me speak again, I say: "Isn't that the point?"

He roars as if the pain, retreating from my body, has slipped across the cell and entered his.

"The point? The *point?*"

He clamps his mouth shut, calms himself. He waves his shackled hand across his face; the chain clinks and settles as he dismisses me.

I look at him then, at his matted filthy hair and beard, at his flesh, bruised and scarred, hanging from his bones like congealed wax from a half-burned candle, kneeling on the bare concrete floor of a cell that still smells of shit and sweat after all this time, a man anticipating nothing but the endless repetition of truth and lies, the relentless narration of plot and counter-plot, of evidence and orders and analyses and situation reports, merely to defer the inevitable metastasis of terror.

I climb the steps to the Crypt, my pain and nausea fading with each step. Warren hands me back Stephen's last journal entry without looking at me, his gesture unconsciously mirroring that of Volorik. He says, "I'm sorry," and I have no idea what he's talking about. He tells me Butler wants to see me in her office. I ask why; he says he is just passing on the message. He says I'd better read the typescript first.

I take the lift to the fourth floor, to my own office, where I shut the door and sit at my desk, facing the picture of the jug, the pearls and the horse-headed dagger. I rummage through the desk drawer looking not for moisturiser, but for the morphine capsules the hospital have given me, but which, until now, I haven't tried. The cancer will kill me one way or another. I thought it would make no difference how much it hurt. I was wrong.

B will say she's sorry, too, and offer me a drink. She will hug me. I will not respond and she will step away without a word. My tumour will be napping, but I'll know it can't be trusted. The morphine will smudge the borders of my body. When she touches me again, a hand on the arm, I will worry that her fingers might press – no, not press – might *settle* a centimetre or so into my flesh.

We will be in Butler's office on the fifth floor, which I have not yet visited. Over the last few years we've met in the observation room of Volorik's interrogation suite, or, occasionally, at her desk on the third floor where she maintains her cover as a member of my team. Her office will be spacious, one window overlooking the river, another giving a broad view downstream to the centre of the city, neither obscured by the heavy, sooty netting required on lower floors. Someone must believe bomb blasts can't reach this high. Barges will silently tug rusting waste containers downstream past government buildings and corporate headquarters and on towards the incinerator plant. Powerful semi-inflatables full of river police and our own plainclothes operatives will carve intricate wakes up and down the surface of the river. Cormorants will bob and dive in the butterscotch water.

She will steer me away from her desk towards the matching sofas set at right angles in a corner of the room, where we can sit side-on, not face-to-face, and talk not to each other but to a neutral point in front of both of us.

She will ask if he ever said anything.

"Oh, yes."

She will wait. The pain in my gut will be bearable.

"He said he was going to kill himself."

She will ask this, and I will say this, even though we'll both know Stephen never actually said those words, but wrote them in his journal, which Warren decoded and she must have read.

"He said it more than once, though. When he was younger. Before he went away to university. Which made me think he probably wouldn't."

"What did you say?"

I hadn't said anything, of course, because I'd never admitted to reading his journal. I will remember something Mary once told me, though, and say:

"What's the rush?"

"You actually said that?"

"I said: Calm down. You can kill yourself any time you like."

"You said that?"

I will nod, although it won't be true.

"Calm down?"

"Yes."

"And?"

"He did."

There will be a pause.

"I mean: he stopped talking about it."

"Which you didn't think might be a danger sign?"

I didn't. And not just because this entire conversation, in which I will find myself participating easily, naturally, with just the right degree of dissociation in my voice, will be imaginary, a fiction Butler and I conspire to create. Because, as far as we both knew, he had written that suicide was cowardly, self-indulgent, and that he had a duty to make the world a better place.

He had been younger, then.

"Next time I'll know the signs," I'll say.

I'll know the absence of a signal is the signal. I'll know it isn't possible to live as if nothing will ever happen, because it will; and I'll know, too, that even if I can't believe anything I do will make a difference, it's not possible to live as if it didn't. Because they're dead. My father, Mary, my daughter. Our daughter.

Stephen isn't dead, but it's not for want of trying.

I will leave Butler's office, leave the Faculty, walk out and down to the river where I will watch litter flow upstream with the tide.

Then I will cross the bridge to the hospital, where I will ask to see my son.

I will resign, even though it is not possible to resign.

When I return home, my neighbours – not the new neighbours, the ones on the other side – will complain about a knocking on the wall. I will tell them about Stephen and they will say they are sorry, sorry for complaining. They will ask how he is now.

I will go back to the doctor, and when I do he will welcome me into his consulting room and I will not object to his avuncular manner. He will say, perhaps, that there is still a chance the right treatment might save my life, and I will not feel the need to say that what he means is: prolong my death. And, after another visit, not the next, but the fourth or fifth, some way down the line, when the radiotherapy is over and the chemo begins to take effect, when I am tired and sick and hairless, Stephen will ask:

"How is it today?"

And I will answer.

# ACKNOWLEDGEMENTS

All books are built out of countless other books, but this one owes an obvious debt to thse nine in particular:

Aeschylus, (trans. Robert Fagles) *The Oresteia*, Penguin, 1981

Saint Augustine (trans. Henry Bettenson), *City of God*, Penguin, 2003

Marcus Aurelius, (trans. Maxwell Staniforth), *Meditations*, Penguin, 1964

Samuel Beckett, *Endgame*, Faber & Faber, 1964.

Emil Cioran, (trans. Richard Howard), *A Short History of Decay*, Penguin, 2010; and *The Trouble with Being Born*, Arcade, 2012

Yasunari Kawabata, (trans. Edward G. Seidensticker) *The Master of Go*, Yellow Jersey Press, 2006

Michel de Montaigne, (trans. John Florio), *Essays*, NYRB, 2014

Mohamedou Ould Slahi, *Guantánamo Diary*, Canongate, 2015

This book has been typeset by
SALT PUBLISHING LIMITED
using Neacademia, a font designed by Sergei Egorov
for the Rosetta Type Foundry in the Czech Republic. It
is manufactured using Holmen Book Cream 70gsm, a
Forest Stewardship Council™ certified paper from the
Hallsta Paper Mill in Sweden. It was printed and bound
by Clays Limited in Bungay, Suffolk, Great Britain.

CROMER
GREAT BRITAIN
MMXIX